Praise for

# YOUNG HOUDINI

## The Magician's Fire

'It's AMAZING! I just couldn't stop reading it, every bit of it is full of adventure and excitement. I loved it!'

**Jaya, age 8**

'*Young Houdini* is so adventurous. It is full of heroes and sinister villains. It is written so well that I can't put the book down.'

**Eva, age 9**

'I really enjoyed *Young Houdini: The Magician's Fire* as it combines magic, dare devil stunts and investigation stories into one. Billie, Harry and Arthur are fun, loveable characters which children will aspire to be like.'

**Hamish, age 11**

# SIMON NICHOLSON

YOUNG HOUDINI

The Magician's Fire

OXFORD
UNIVERSITY PRESS

# OXFORD
## UNIVERSITY PRESS

Great Clarendon Street, Oxford OX2 6DP
Oxford University Press is a department of the University of Oxford.
It furthers the University's objective of excellence in research, scholarship,
and education by publishing worldwide. Oxford is a registered trade mark of
Oxford University Press in the UK and in certain other countries

Database right Oxford University Press (maker)

First published 2015

British Library Cataloguing in Publication Data
Data available

ISBN: 978-0-19-273474-7

1 3 5 7 9 10 8 6 4 2
Printed in Great Britain

Paper used in the production of this book is a natural,
recyclable product made from wood grown in sustainable forests.
The manufacturing process conforms to the environmental
regulations of the country of origin.

*To Olive, Eliza and Roxy*
*May they know no fear*

# Author's Note

Harry Houdini was a magician and escape artist like no other. At the dawn of the twentieth century he travelled the globe, subjecting himself to spectacular and terrifying ordeals, the likes of which had simply never been seen before.

He escaped from nailed-shut crates thrown to the bottom of icy lakes. He writhed his way out of a straitjacket while dangling from a seventy-metre-high bridge. Lashed to the front of a loaded cannon, he sprung from the ropes just before the fuse detonated. Incarcerated by Europe's most ruthless police force in their cruellest prison, he mocked them by walking miraculously free. Nothing defeated him—and no one could explain his mysterious powers.

Who was Harry Houdini and how did he acquire such phenomenal skills? I couldn't stop thinking about what might have happened to him as a boy to turn him into such an extraordinary man.

All great stories have a great beginning. This is the story of Houdini: the boy magician.

Manhattan, 1886

# Chapter 1

The train was coming. Harry could see the puffs of blackened steam rising over a row of broken-down houses. He could hear the clatter of the engine. Down by his feet vibrations were wobbling along the iron rails and the ragged hems of his trousers were wobbling too. *Won't be long now.* He stood there a little longer, his boot polish-stained fingers twitching, his eyes narrowing in the direction of the thundering roar.

He tugged a sturdy-looking padlock out of his jacket pocket and carried on chaining himself to the spot in the middle of the track.

'You've really lost it this time, Harry!'

'Harry! Are you absolutely sure about this?'

A boy and a girl stood just a few paces away. Billie, the girl, wore a ragged, glue-spattered factory smock, and she was casually leaning against a concrete stump, her head on one side, an eyebrow raised. *Typical, not even the tiniest bit impressed,* thought Harry with a smile, glancing across at the boy, who was a far more satisfying sight. Arthur was completely beside himself with excitement, hopping from foot to foot, his neatly tailored tweed suit flapping, his hands racing through a copy of the *New York City Train Timetable.*

'Do you really think this is a good idea, Harry? My calculations have turned out right, you see.' Stitches popped in the tweed suit and the younger boy's tie swirled as he flung an arm towards the puffs of smoke. 'That's the 15:24 from Grand Central. Which by my estimate is due to hit this exact spot . . .' He tugged a fob-watch from his waistcoat, dangled it in front of his face, and stared at it with eyes the size of half-dollar coins. 'In exactly two minutes, twenty-seven seconds' time!'

'So we have to hurry, Artie!' Harry looped a chain around his left leg, pulled it up round his head, and adjusted it so that it was at a jaunty angle. He heard his voice echo around, still full of the accent of his far-away Hungarian home, so different from his friend's English tones. 'Good job on the calculations but I'm not even properly manacled yet! Another chain, Billie?'

'One of the real heavy ones? Or perhaps something a little lighter, *sir?*' Another grin, and Billie pushed off the concrete stump, reached into the sack at her feet, and yanked out a clinking length of iron. 'I managed to find you a nice selection, heavy ones, light ones, that sort of thing . . .' Her voice bounced along with drawls and twangs as she swung the chain about a bit. 'Any other deadly situations you'd like me and Artie to rustle up for you? Dangle you by a rope off Brooklyn Bridge? Or smuggle you into the lion's cage at the City Zoo, maybe? We're getting pretty good now, I'm sure we could fix it . . .'

'You'd do a great job, both of you, but can we talk about it later?' Harry wrapped the chain around his middle, making sure that it too was at a jaunty angle. 'Let's just concentrate on the Great Train—'

'The Great Train Escape, I know.' Billie's left eyebrow lifted a little higher. 'Hey Artie, seeing as we're busy with trains today, did I ever tell you about my own brush with one? The Louisiana Express Hay Wagon Ride, that's what I call it, and it was pretty rough—'

'There's no time, Billie!' Harry slid the padlock through the links.

'Sure there's time! So, I was desperate for a ride and so I hung out on a bridge near a goods station, waiting. When the train rattled underneath with a load of wagons of hay, I just jumped down! Nearly broke a leg!' Billie reached behind her back, pulled round the little ukulele she kept strapped there, and started strumming a tune. 'But that's what it's like on the road, you've got to grab any chance you can. So there I was, riding all the way to Arkansas, strumming my uke and—'

'Billie! Not now! Everyone's waiting. Look!'

Harry snapped the padlock shut and managed to jerk his head towards the rabble of about fifteen people lined up along the top of the bank on the far side of the tracks, framed against the blue September sky. Passers-by, shopkeepers, and even a couple of washer-women—Billie and Arthur had spent nearly an hour drumming them up by racing around the surrounding streets, and every one of them seemed gripped by what was going on, their gazes fixed in his direction. *They'll stare even harder now,* Harry thought, as he plucked the key from the padlock and sent it flying through the air. It vanished into a patch of thorny bushes some distance away.

'You've really done it now.' Billie's ukulele playing stopped. Even she was looking impressed, staring after the key.

'Exactly!' Harry jerked his head towards the crowd. 'That's what everyone's thinking!'

'Yes, but you really *have* done it!' Arthur was a high-speed hopping, page-flicking, watch-waggling blur. 'We'll never be able to find it in all those thorns!'

'It's all part of the act.' Harry breathed deeply, and stared at the padlock as hard as he could. 'Look, I shouldn't really be talking—I'm meant to be pretending to have magical powers.'

He carried on doing just that. The clattering roar was louder now, the rails were vibrating faster, his ragged trouser-hems were flapping faster too, but he didn't bother about any of those things. Instead, he carried on staring at the chains with that deliberately mysterious gaze. He even tugged the padlock up to his mouth and muttered to it. *See a boy free himself through the speaking of ancient charms*, that was what Billie and Arthur had told the crowd—and, from the excited gasps he could hear drifting from the bank, it sounded like his audience was well on the way to believing it too. He kept muttering to the padlock, deliberately using phrases of Hungarian, knowing that the unfamiliar words would sound particularly mysterious to the listening crowd. He muttered even louder, and made his eyes roll about, pretending to lose himself completely in a magical trance, even as he detected faint odours of oil and soot, curling up his nose . . .

'The train! The train!'

Harry's eyes stopped rolling. They flicked towards the crowd. Every one of those fifteen heads had swivelled to the left because the train had shot out from behind the houses and was curving steadily around the track. Arms pointed, faces turned white. The engine, a hurtling bulk of iron, was still several hundred yards away, but steam shrieked from it as it clanged along the rails, and it was gathering speed. Harry watched it. The odours of oil and soot weren't just curling up his nose now, they were snaking down into his mouth, flavouring the spit trickling down his throat. *Time to get a move on.* But he couldn't resist squeezing in just a bit more bug-eyed magical staring at the chains.

'Harry! You've left it too late!'

A yell from Arthur as he raced for the thorny bushes. Billie was pulling off a well-rehearsed swoon, tottering about with the back of a hand against her forehead. *Nicely done,* thought Harry, as he watched Billie collapse onto the gravel; meanwhile Artie arrived at the bush and started rooting about as if all was lost. *All part of the act.* Still, they had been right earlier— there *wasn't* any way they could find the key and run back to set him free before the train hit. The thought made the chains holding him in place feel particularly heavy. Under his threadbare shirt, he felt a drop of sweat glide down between his shoulder blades. *Yes, time to get a move on . . .*

'Stop the train!'

'Somebody DO something!'

Screams from the crowd. One of the washer-women had dropped her basket, the clothes inside tumbling down the bank, but no one seemed to have noticed. *Utterly gripped.* More drops of sweat were gathering now, on his forehead, his neck, under his arms, and Harry could feel strange little twitches quivering through his body. *Good*—every twitch, every drop of sweat would help him concentrate on the trick that lay ahead.

He lifted the padlock to his mouth again and muttered a bit more of that spell. He surrounded the padlock with his hands so no one would see the tiny bulge in his upper lip as his tongue curled up inside. Harry closed his eyes and felt his tongue deftly fetch down the little bent nail that was lodged there and nudge it around until it was gripped between his teeth. The bent end poked out of the corner of his mouth and he shot it into the padlock's keyhole.

*Concentrate.*

Harry tilted his head. He had carefully bent the nail so it fitted the padlock perfectly. He had practised endless times, first with his hands, then with his mouth. But he still felt his jaw shudder slightly as it shifted so that the nail angled upwards. His brain throbbed with the clatter of iron wheels, the shriek of steam. *Concentrate, concentrate.* He stared straight at the train, just a hundred yards away now, as he carried on picking the lock. And then the nail slipped.

Unexpectedly, the padlock had jerked to the left, tugging the nail from his teeth. For a couple of seconds, the little length of metal balanced precariously on his lower lip. He felt his whole body turn cold as he tried, with his tongue, to fetch it back. His vision blurred and he realized that his eyes had crossed, struggling to hold the nail in view as it balanced such a short distance away. His tongue strained, the twitches raced through every part of him.

*Concentrate.*

The nail was back between his teeth. He shot it back into the lock again, his jaw re-angling. He checked the train, which had jammed on its brakes but was hurtling forward anyway, an iron blur, just forty yards away. *Thirty, twenty.* The brakes screeched but all he could hear was, from deep inside the padlock, the stretching of tiny springs, the grind of tiny levers.

Then, echoing out of the keyhole, a click.

The clasp sprang open. The chains, heavy and cold, slithered away from him. One of them snagged on his left elbow but he shook it off, shaking off the other chains too, sending them flying away from the track. He looked up and saw the train's vast front, racing up to him. His legs, he had to admit, were a little less steady than usual, but he managed to spring into the air, just in time, and thudded onto the gravel next to the tracks.

He tucked the nail back inside his lip. Briefly, he remembered that troubling moment when it had dangled so precariously, and took in a shaky breath. But then he jumped up, brushing the dust from his clothes. He stumbled away from the track, his ragged clothes billowing in the thundering breeze of the train's wagons as they clattered past, picking up speed again. Ahead of him was the crowd. Everyone was clapping, cheering, waving hats in the air, throwing coins in his direction; Harry stopped walking and stood there for some time, watching the coins land. The train was gone now, but he still stood there. His vision blurred, and for a while he stopped thinking of anything apart from his still-pounding heart, his still-trembling body. Then he felt something jab him in his side.

'Harry? We are *here*, you know?'

It was Billie. She was standing next to him, laughing, and it was her elbow that was doing the jabbing, quite hard. Harry blinked, and then looked round at Arthur, who was on his other side, a smile on his face too.

'Sorry.' Harry blinked again, and felt his face grow warm. 'Sometimes takes me a bit of time to come round . . .'

'Don't worry, we're used to it.' Billie rolled her eyes.

'Thanks.' Harry held out his hands. 'So anyway—let's give them what they want, shall we?'

He waited for his friends to grab his hands. Then, together with them, he performed the move that he had practised more than any other.

A slow, elegant bow.

# Chapter 2

Harry ran across the park. Light was just starting to fade from the sky, and the last wisps of soot and engine oil had cleared from his clothes. His boots thudded over the cool grass and a wooden shoeshine box swung from his shoulder, rattling with the cans and brushes inside. Flipping open the box's lid, he checked one of its compartments and snapped the lid shut again. Leaping over a railing, he took a shortcut through a flower bed, ran across another stretch of grass and joined Billie, hiding behind a rhododendron bush.

'Is it ready, Harry?'

'Sure is!'

'Exactly the way we ordered it? Every last detail?'

'Every last one! Good thing the train trick went down so well just now, we'd never have had enough otherwise.' He tugged out the lining of his trouser pocket, empty of coins. 'That's got to be the craziest trick yet, yeah?'

'You bet, Harry, no doubt about it.' Billie peered back through the bush. 'He's still in there, by the way. Hasn't come out since we said goodbye.'

Harry joined her peering through the twigs and leaves. A short distance away, a brilliant white building towered beside the park, its windows shining, marble steps running up to its front door. Harry checked the windows, inspecting them for any sign of movement inside. But, as usual, the whole house was eerily still.

'So how did you find out, Billie?' Harry turned back. 'That it's his birthday, I mean.'

'Mentioned it to me a couple of months ago. "The seventeenth September", he said, and that's today.'

'But how come he didn't say anything earlier? The train, that's all he wanted to talk about!'

'He loves our tricks, doesn't he? Probably grateful we were doing one—must have helped take his mind off it. Still, his mind'll be back on it now. Wait, there he is!'

Harry peered again. Billie was right—the front door was opening, and Arthur was stepping out. And she was right about something else too—Arthur's mind was clearly no longer on anything to do with their tricks. The younger boy's movements were slow and his head was lowered as he trod down the steps, wandered down the sidewalk, and crossed the street into the park. Harry even heard a faint sigh drifting through the air. He glanced at Billie, who nodded, and, just as Arthur reached the bush, they strolled out.

'Hi Artie!'

'Billie? Harry?' Artie stopped, and blinked at them. 'I thought you were both working this evening.'

'Turns out I'm not due at the factory just yet.' Billie adjusted her cap, which was every bit as glue-spattered as her smock. 'And you're not planning to shine any shoes for the next couple of hours or so either, are you Harry?'

'Thought I'd leave it a while,' said Harry, shrugging.

'Oh.' Arthur looked puzzled. 'Well, I'm not doing anything very exciting, I'm afraid. Just going for a quick walk round the park. Before . . .' He stared back at the house. 'Going back inside again.'

'We'll go for a walk with you, Artie.' Billie tugged his arm. 'Come on.'

They set off across the park. Billie reached for her ukulele, strung across her back as usual, but seemed to change her mind, and Harry knew why. She, like him, had seen the first signs of that familiar kink forming on their friend's forehead. At the same time, Arthur's left hand was reaching down to his jacket pocket, drawing out a little ribbon of paper with letters and dots running along it. Harry kept walking, and tried to think of what to say.

'Heading off to Chicago, is he?' Billie got there first. 'Like you expected?'

'First thing tomorrow.' Arthur ran a finger along the dots. 'He sent this message through from his office yesterday, telling the servants. The machine in the hallway hammered it out, along with the usual stuff about stocks and shares. Servants read it and left it in the wastepaper bin, as usual.'

'I just don't get it.' Billie put her hand on Arthur's shoulder. 'He's only just got back from a trip to . . . where was it again?'

'Washington,' said Arthur. 'He was gone three weeks.'

'I mean, one thing to spend all your time in an office in the city where you actually live—but travelling all over the country?' Billie shook her head.

'He's got meetings, hasn't he? That's what it's like if you come to America to set up a brand new bank.' Arthur frowned. 'It's been this way ever since we moved to New York, and that's eight months now. Mind you, he totally ignored me in London too. As long as I can remember, he's been just the same. Work comes first, a nice expensive house comes second, and having a bunch of servants who do exactly what he wants is important too.' He swung back towards the house. 'Me, I'm just expected to tag along.'

His eyes narrowed. Harry swung round too, and saw why. As daylight faded, lamps were being lit inside the grand front room of the brilliant white building. Inside, stood the figure of Lord Trilby-Roberts, Arthur's father. Tall, stiff and wearing an immaculately tailored suit, the rich banker was standing perfectly straight and talking on a telephone, staring out through the window with an expression that, even at this distance, seemed cold and aloof. Around him, various servants busily gathered papers and files, no doubt in preparation for the trip to Chicago.

'So he's just going to leave you again?' Harry turned back. 'To hang around in that house?'

'Along with all his other stuff.' Artie kept staring at the window. 'Antique furniture, clocks from Switzerland, that sort of thing.'

'Good thing he installed the ticker-tape machine,' Billie said. 'Least that way you get warning of what he's planning.'

'I know,' said Arthur. 'I know.'

He reached back into his pocket and drew out another ribbon, gripping its end with particular force.

'Actually, the machine hammered out another message this morning.' His hand tightened until the knuckles were white. 'Something I wasn't expecting—today of all days.'

'Really?' Billie, peering at the ribbon, looked hopeful.

'Found it crumpled up in the bin, just like the others. Do the servants really think I won't find them?'

'It was from your father in his office? To the servants back home?'

'Of course.'

'And it arrived today? The seventeenth of September?'

'Yes.'

'And it's about you?'

'Certainly is.'

'So what is it? What does it say?'

'It's instructions to the servants about contacting another boarding school,' said Arthur, and he crumpled the ribbon into a tiny hard ball. His eyes were curiously bright as his thumb and finger gripped the tiny paper ball. Harry wasn't sure what to say at all and neither, from the look of her, was Billie.

'Boarding school?' She managed something, at last. 'Sounds grim. Still, at least that's taking *some* kind of interest in you . . .'

'Not really. There are different sorts of boarding schools, for a start. The one Father has in mind is the sort of place you send someone if you specifically intend to take no interest in them whatsoever for as long as you possibly can. Hard for me to be even the tiniest distraction to him if I've been sent miles away.' Arthur held up the ball of paper, and glared at it. 'The school's in Dayton, Ohio. So that's 452 miles away, to be precise.'

'So what are you going to do?' Billie looked genuinely worried. 'We don't want you disappearing anywhere, Artie.'

'Me neither. What, and not see the two people who *do* actually take an interest in me? I don't think so.' Artie flicked the ball furiously away. 'I'll use the normal tricks. I've foiled all the other attempts to send me away and I'll foil this one too, don't you worry. It's just it's a bit much, him doing this. On my . . . On my b . . .'

He stopped. He sat down on a bench, hard. The paper ball was bouncing down the path, and he stared after it, his hands shoved in his tweed trouser pockets. *As bad as we've ever seen him*, thought Harry, and he turned back to the white house again. The tall, rigid figure was still there, the telephone in his hand, his servants bustling obediently around him. Harry's eyes narrowed, just as his friend's had done. Then he turned back to Billie who, with a determined look on her face, had plonked herself down on the bench, right next to Arthur.

'Don't worry, Artie.' She thumped him on the shoulder. 'We've got you a birthday treat. Pass the blindfold, Harry!'

'Birthday—how d'you know it was my birthday? OOF!'

The blindfold was out of Harry's shoeshine box. A perfectly clean rag, he had bought it specially, and he swiftly pulled it over Arthur's eyes and knotted it round the back of his head. Arthur's hands flailed as Billie hoisted him over her shoulder and staggered off across the park.

'Where are you taking me? What's going on—HEY! That tickles!'

'You've always said you wanted to be a magician's assistant!' Harry ran on ahead. 'Wearing the occasional blindfold's part of it. Ready to row, Billie?'

He jumped into the little boat moored at the edge of the pond. Billie tottered up to it and Harry helped her in, catching Arthur and propping him on one of the seats. Billie leaped in, grabbed an oar, and Harry grabbed one too. Together, they started to row, picking up speed quickly and passing various ducks.

'What IS going on?' Arthur, still blindfolded, was laughing now.

'You're in the hands of an expert, birthday boy.' Billie sculled to the left. 'Not as if I haven't blindfolded someone before. Tied her up too! The owner of my orphanage, down in New Orleans!'

'You've told us this, Billie!' Harry rowed faster.

'Now that was a real rough business, and I'd only just got started then—the Knotted Sheet Dangle, that's what I call it! Not only did I have to deal with the scariest owner of an orphanage there ever was, next I had to jump out the window and climb down a rope of knotted sheets, all the way down to the street below and—WATCH OUT!'

The boat thudded into the side. Harry threw the mooring rope, lassoed the mooring post, and helped Billie pull Arthur out. It was Harry's turn to hoist the younger boy onto his shoulder now, and he stumbled out through the park gate and tottered onto a horse-drawn omnibus. He and Billie sat down, and for the next twenty minutes they clattered across Manhattan, watching the city shudder past the window, laughing at the odd looks the other passengers were giving them, two scruffy street kids with a blindfolded boy in a tweed suit squashed between them. The omnibus tilted to a halt, and together they hoisted up their friend and carried him out onto the street. On the other side, they saw their destination.

A small, rather grimy-looking diner.

They burst in through the door, the bell somersaulting above them. They carried Arthur to a table, propped him on a chair, and drew up chairs of their own. Harry nodded to a waitress, who rattled a little wooden trolley across. She picked up what was upon it and lowered it onto the table. At the same moment, Harry and Billie removed Arthur's blindfold.

'Happy Birthday, Artie!'

A cake. Chocolate icing spiralled on its sides. Cream oozed from its centre, spilling onto the plate, and three layers of sponge could be detected, each one sitting on a thick layer of yet more icing. Artie, blinking as his eyes adjusted to the light, took in all these details, but one seemed to affect him in particular: written on the cake's top in sugary sprinkles was his name, along with a skilfully iced picture of a stack of interesting-looking books.

'But how did you afford this?' Arthur gasped.

'The money from the trick, silly,' Billie replied.

'But . . . that's Harry's money, really. He stood in front of th—'

'That's not how we do things, Artie, you know that,' Harry interrupted. 'You calculated the train time, didn't you? Billie found the chains, and both of you ran round drumming up that crowd . . .'

'With no crowd, there wouldn't *be* any money,' agreed Billie, grabbing a spoon.

'Exactly. So we split the cash three ways.' Harry leaned forward and jabbed a finger on the table-cloth. 'Anyway, who knows where I'd have got with my tricks if it hadn't been for you encouraging me, Artie. Remember when you saw me trying to cross Sixth Avenue by leaping between speeding streetcars? Might have gone nowhere, that. Just some shoeshine boy, leaping about—no one else was noticing. But then you wandered up and told me all about that book you'd been reading in the library . . .'

'*Fire Dances in the Amazon*,' said Arthur, quietly.

'Magicians there prove their skills by dancing through pits of fire! Why not do the same, flying through the showers of sparks from the streetcars?' Harry turned to Billie, his finger still firm on the tablecloth. 'Same goes for you, Billie. You saw me prac-tising tightrope-walking along the back of that park bench . . .'

'Waved my arms around, trying to make you lose balance.' Billie smiled.

'Like I say, at least you noticed. And you also had the idea of stringing a rope way up high between two trees, and getting me to walk along it while mutter-ing spells and wriggling my arms free of no less than twenty-five knots, helped me practise it over and over too, and *that* was how we drew our first crowd.' The finger was hurting now from all the jabbing. 'So anyway, that's why we split stuff in three. And because it's your birthday, Artie, me and Billie decided to spend our shares on something you'd like.'

'So that just left your bit. And we decided to throw that in too, if that's all right by you?' Billie added.

'Yes, of course . . .' Arthur's voice had gone very quiet indeed. 'Thanks, folks . . .'

For some time, he said nothing more. He just sat there, staring at the cake. Harry, uncertain what to do next, didn't move either. The silence went on for so long that the top layer of the cake, the icing melting beneath it, had begun to tilt to one side. Harry and Billie exchanged worried looks. Then, finally, Arthur reached out a hand, and picked up the knife.

'Father can ignore me as much as he likes, and send as many messages about boarding schools too.' He smiled. 'The three of us—we've got some serious eating to do.'

The cake flew apart. Arthur cut the first slice, and then cut two more for Billie and Harry, and then kept on cutting more slices for all three of them, in between gobbling down what was on his plate. Spoons flashed, hands grabbed, bits of sponge bounced across the table, and Harry saw one of the customers at a nearby table duck as a blob of icing hurtled by him. No more slices were left, just a few crumbs and smears of icing, and these were busily devoured as well, Billie even holding her plate up to her face and rotating it so that her tongue could lick up every last trace. At last, they were done, and they tilted back their chairs and wiped a few last smears from their mouths.

'Deee-licious!' said Billie.

'The best cake I've ever tasted.' Arthur nodded. 'And it's the best birthday I can remember as well.'

'And that, Artie,' said Harry, leaning back in his chair furthest of all. 'Was well worth standing in front of a hurtling train for!'

He meant every word. He had meant the words earlier too. And he wasn't the only one who felt that way, it seemed, because just then he felt his hand grow warm, and realized that Arthur had taken hold of it. The tweed-suited boy took hold of Billie's hand too, and then Billie reached across and grabbed the only hand that remained on the table, Harry's other one. The three of them sat there, the business of the diner clattering around them. No trace of sadness on Artie's face now, it was smiling all over, and Billie was smiling as well, and Harry felt his own face break into a grin too . . .

His eyes flicked up to the diner's clock. Then to the grimy window. Through it, a familiar spindly shape could be seen, hovering by a lamp post.

'Your birthday treat's not over yet, Artie!' Harry scraped back his chair. 'It's only just beginning!'

'Really?' Arthur looked about, confused.

'I think *I* know what Harry's talking about.' Billie, turning, could clearly see the spindly shape too.

'Seen him? Seen who?' Arthur swivelled round in his seat, trying to see.

'Herbie,' said Harry. 'He came!'

# Chapter 3

Harry, Arthur and Billie raced across the street, towards the elderly figure by the lamp post.

'Hello Herbie!'

The old man turned round. His grey hair drooped, his movements were slow, and his clothes billowed around his limbs as he gripped his walking cane. Harry leaped onto the kerb, balanced there, and waited for the complicated wrinkles of Herbie's face to arrange themselves into a smile.

'Harry.' There it was. 'Half past six, just as we agreed.'

'Did you bring the tickets? It's Artie's birthday, remember.'

'Of course.' The smile hung there, as three rect-angular stubs of card flowered in Herbie's hand. He handed them over, and started walking slowly down the street, his cane tapping. 'Three tickets for tonight's performance. I assume you wish to watch me for the usual reason?'

'You bet, Mr Lemster.' Billie hurried up, Arthur just behind. 'Why else would Harry want to see a magician, eh?'

'Maybe we could go into the theatre with you? Seeing as it's my birthday?' Arthur walked along, trying to sound innocent. 'Just to have a look backstage . . .'

'Ah, that would be quite against the rules, Arthur.' The old man gripped his cane. 'I never let anyone behind the curtain, you know that. You won't attempt to meet me at the stage door after the show either, I trust?' He stopped. 'That is our agreement. What if your keen eyes spotted some trace of a trick, a clue, that might remain upon me? That would be most unfair . . .'

'Harry'd be looking, that's for sure.' Arthur nodded. 'He's seen a whole bunch of other magicians since we last met, Herbie— Chinese conjurers, Russian tricksters, Indian illusionists, you name them. Discovered something from pretty much every one of them too . . .'

'*Stole*, you mean,' said Billie, laughing.

'Oh it's not stealing, young Billie.' Another smile from Herbie. 'It's the whole business of trickery. A game that's been going on nearly a thousand years,

I'd say. We magicians, we're all studying each other, watching each other, keenly hunting for the slightest clue, the slightest trace of each other's devices. The flick of a thumb? The dart of an arm? An ingeniously placed trapdoor? Whatever it is, if we find it fair and square, it's ours to use.' A scratching sound from his pocket, and his hand rose, a flaming match gripped between finger and thumb. '*The Game*, we call it. And young Harry's got the knack for it.'

'Sure do.' Harry watched as the flame quadrupled in size, and then flew into the magician's mouth. He also saw the tiny flutter of a finger, which snuffed out the flame just as the lips closed. 'I spotted that trick first time I met you, Herbie.'

'Ah, but perhaps I saw you looking?' The old magician winked as he drew the match, flaming even more brightly, out of his ear. 'Perhaps I spotted you in the crowd, with your ragged clothes and shoeshine box? Perhaps I observed, from the shape of your face and the accent in your voice, that you might come from the east of Europe too, a region most famous for its tricksters and illusionists?' Another wink. 'Perhaps I decided to angle myself so that you saw the device. To introduce you to the world of magic and all that it can be . . .'

'Doesn't explain how I picked it up so quick.' Down by his side, Harry's fingers were twitching, mimicking the device, that deft finger-flutter, and his body flinched too, as he remembered the time of that first meeting, in the middle of last winter, just a few weeks after he had arrived in New York. A penniless shoeshine boy, that was all he had been then, without a friend in the whole city, struggling to earn a living on the freezing sidewalks . . . 'Stayed up late that night, practising the trick and woke up with a few scorch marks on my lips the next morning. Right away, I started doing it! Bit of a shock for the gents whose shoes I was shining, to look down and see . . . Herbie?'

He peered closely at the old man. He always seemed a bit frail, but this was something different. Herbie's collar was damp with sweat, even though the evening air was perfectly cool, and the tips of his fingers were trembling. Tiny signs, and neither Billie and Arthur seemed to have noticed them, but Harry had, and he tried to look for more, only to find the old magician staring straight back at him. The trembling stopped, and Herbie Lemster's eyes started flicking over Harry instead.

'Miraculously escaped from an oncoming train, did we?' The old man walked on.

'How'd you know that?' Billie butted in.

'Faint bruising around Harry's wrists, Billie. Some tightly looped chains, I'll wager . . .' Herbie lifted a finger, almost steady now, and pointed. 'Although the main clue is the distinct smell of engine oil drifting from young Harry's clothes, mingling with the usual boot polish. Given that, and knowing our young friend's tastes for excitement . . .' He managed a smile. 'Spotting little clues, tiny traces—that's what we magicians are good at, you see.'

'He only just got away with it, Mr Lemster!' Arthur said. 'The crowd went totally wild!'

'Ah yes, the threat of genuine danger . . .' Herbie nodded, his cane tapping ahead of him. 'Mind you, danger can enter a magician's life in so many ways . . .'

Something was definitely up. The old man's fingers were trembling again, and more perspiration gleamed on his skin, and these signs seemed to become even more pronounced, Harry observed, the further Herbie shuffled along the street. Glancing across at Billie and Arthur, he saw that they had noticed Herbie's distress too, because they had fallen silent and were staring at the old man closely. Reaching the end of the street, turning the corner, Herbie covered the last few yards towards the rickety old building, looming across the street.

The Wesley Jones Theatre. Its walls crumbled, its windows were lop-sided, and faded posters hung on its hoardings, advertising its regular acts, one of which was a certain Herbie Lemster, Magician. An excited crowd was already gathered outside, forming a queue to buy tickets, as Harry watched his elderly friend, heading off towards the theatre's stage door.

'Mr Lemster?' Billie called out after him. 'Are you feeling all right?'

He swung round to face them. No question that something was up now. His clothes shuddered, drops of sweat gathered in those complicated wrinkles, and Herbie's face had turned strangely pale. And yet, obvious though those signs were, the words the old magician said next did nothing to explain them, or even acknowledge that they existed.

'Good luck . . . Good luck with the world of magic . . .' he stammered, eyes wide and shimmering. 'And all that it can be . . .'

And with that, the old man turned, and disappeared into the Wesley Jones Theatre.

# Chapter 4

Harry sat down in the theatre. The insides were dilapidated, the seats broken, the curtain grubby and
moth-eaten, but the audience was bustling and excited,
waiting to see their favourite acts. Harry dropped his
shoeshine box down by his feet and prepared to go
to work which, given what had just happened, wasn't
going to be very easy.

'So what do you think's up with him?' Billie
dropped into the next seat, and kicked her boots up
onto the back of the one in front. 'He looked really
odd.'

'I hope he's all right.' Arthur settled himself too.
'Herbie got you started, Harry. If he hadn't done that,
maybe none of us would have met.'

'It's true.' Billie turned to Harry. 'You might never
have practised tightrope-walking on that park bench,
and I've never have picked you out.'

'Same for me and the streetcar-jumping stuff.' Arthur nodded.

'It could all be part of the act. Herbie could be putting it on deliberately, as a distraction.' Harry had cobbled this explanation together on the way in, and he was trying to get used to it. 'He's planning that I'll worry about that, and miss any little clue that might give his tricks away. It's pretty clever of ol' Herbie, if you think about it.'

His friends looked at him. Billie's eyebrows were raised pretty high and Arthur was frowning, but at least they weren't saying he was flat wrong. Maybe his explanation wasn't a bad one after all, and Harry decided to carry on as if that was the case. *The Game.* Adjusting his position, he prepared to observe the old man's act.

'By the way, Artie, have you thought any more about what you said yesterday? My new name?'

'Ah, yes.' Still looking worried, Arthur adjusted his tie as the lights sputtered out. 'A fair number of magicians invent themselves a new one. Something that catches the attention . . .'

'Had any more ideas?'

'I was doing some research earlier today, actually,' Arthur continued. 'Magicians sometimes name themselves after really famous magicians from long ago—that way they grab some of their reputation. Now there's this old French magician, very famous when he was alive, called Jean Robert-Houdin . . .'

'Bit of a mouthful,' Billie commented. 'And Harry doesn't speak a word of French.'

'Yes, but you could make it shorter. And change it a bit, so it's more like a name in Hungarian, which Harry obviously does speak. So *Houdin*. Stick an 'i' on the end—*Houdini*.'

'Interesting—' Harry began, but by then the curtain was rising. Prettily dressed ladies sang songs, acrobats tumbled, and Harry sat with his friends, watching the show. A new act followed, in which dancers pretended to be pearl divers, floating in front of a rippling blue backcloth as if under the sea. Harry enjoyed that too, even though he immediately spotted the wires that held the dancers up, and saw that the huge shark was just a shadow. The other acts trooped on, some Cossack dancers, a man who told jokes while dressed as a parrot, the pearl divers again, and then a leopardskin-wearing strongman called Bruno, who made three of the prettily dressed ladies sit on a chair and lifted it. Another wire, Harry observed. But then Herbie appeared, and Harry leaned forward, concentrating.

The tiniest twitch of Herbie's trouser pocket, the faintest bulge of a sleeve, the tilt of a shoe could give something away. Harry glanced down at his hands, at his knees, at the whole of his body. Any minute now, bits of it would start twitching to life, practising and mimicking whatever intriguing new move was about to be discovered.

'Ladies and gentlemen . . .' The old man bowed before the crowd. 'Observe . . .'

From out of his jacket, he took a large knife. At speed, he peeled a potato with it, proving it was razor-sharp. Then he tossed it high in the air and, as it plummeted back down, he held out a bare hand and caught it blade first between thumb and finger. No blood on the stage, no injury of any kind. Dazzling enough, but then other knives started hurtling towards the old magician from the back of the theatre, from the boxes, from the wings of the stage, only for Herbie to catch them, one by one, in his frail bare hands. The audience gasped and he held the knives aloft, looking up at their glinting steel. Harry leaned even further forward in his seat, searching for a clue.

But all he could see was that Herbie was trembling again. The old man had held it together during the trick, but now that the applause was thundering around him he was giving way, his clothes shuddering, his wrinkles glittering in the light as perspiration coursed along them. Harry glanced at his friends and saw that they had noticed too, their faces staring worriedly in the dark.

It was like that for the rest of the act. Herbie performed his flower trick, in which not only did a flower grow out of his open hand, but a huge tropical spider scampered out, danced around the flower, and disappeared in a puff of smoke. Impossible to work out, but Harry wasn't even trying now, too distracted by the return of the trembling. Next the old man shut himself in a large crate, a crate that was crushed flat as a large sack of stage weights plummeted down onto it, only for Herbie to shuffle in from the wings unharmed. Normally he walked in quite confidently, but there was no sign of that tonight, it seemed as if he could hardly walk at all, staying right at the edge of the stage, clinging to the proscenium arch for support. Finally, Herbie performed his floating trick, rising into the air and drifting off over a bed of vicious-looking spikes, moving his legs as if he was pedalling a bicycle. But still Harry found it impossible to concentrate, too troubled by the terrible paleness of the old man's face as he cycled off into the gloom.

The curtain flew down. The audience clapped, hooted, stamped. The curtain rose again, with the performers taking a bow, and then it lowered for good. The audience started shuffling out. But Harry remained in his seat, perfectly still, and Billie and Arthur were motionless too.

'I suppose you could be right about Herbie's behaviour being a distraction, Harry,' said Arthur, after a while. 'But it seems unlikely.'

'Completely unlikely,' said Billie.

'I agree,' said Harry. What was up with Herbie? What was this strange weakness that seemed to be taking him over? Harry's fingers drummed on the rickety arms of the theatre seat.

'Come on, we'll find him outside. He'll be leaving by the stage door.'

'But that's against our agreement.' Arthur looked uncertain. 'He doesn't want us to meet him there, he's always said—'

'That's about us discovering his tricks! This is different—we're making sure he's all right! Come on!'

Harry sprang up, his shoeshine box flying up with him. He vaulted over the back of the seats, leaving Arthur and Billie floundering behind. Marching up the aisle towards the foyer doors, he noticed the only other member of the audience who had lingered behind.

A bulky figure, swathed in a dark cape. He was hunched over a briefcase, an arm delving inside it. The face that glanced up at Harry had an oiled and curling red moustache, two piercing eyes, and a long thin nose. On the collar of a cape, a silver brooch with a snake spiralled around a silver sword. From the briefcase, a wisp of purple smoke.

*Odd.* Harry's pace slowed. But Billie and Arthur were hurrying up the aisle behind him and slammed into his back. *Need to find Herbie,* he thought, as he snatched his gaze away from the strange figure, and swept on, out of the theatre.

# Chapter 5

'Follow me!' Harry called back.

'We're trying!' Billie spluttered.

'Ow!' Arthur gasped.

Harry ducked between people's legs in the crowd. A fair chunk of the audience was already bustling around the stage door and there was no chance of him being able to push his way through so he had dropped to the ground and was crawling instead. Angling his shoeshine box through with him, he saw, further back, his friends trying to follow. Arthur was tangled up in a lady's dress; Billie was squashed between two heavy-looking suitcases.

'Stuck! This is like the Tennessee Stagecoach Squeeze! Bumped the whole journey on the stage-coach roof, jammed between two suitcases.' Billie tried to pull herself loose. 'I thought that was bad but—'

'Hurry, Billie!' Harry reached back, grabbed her

hand, and tugged. She lurched forward, but then snagged her smock on a nearby boot's riding spur and got stuck again, while Arthur was still trying to free himself from the dress.

*They'll catch up*, thought Harry, and he wriggled onwards until, at last, he popped out of the crowd, right by the stage door.

'The performers will be emerging soon! Autographs will be available—all included in the price of your ticket, naturally!' A plump gentleman with a flamboyant pink top hat squashed onto his head was bustling about before the crowd. Harry recognized him from his previous visits to the theatre, when he had seen him in the foyer welcoming the audience as they arrived—Mr Wesley Jones himself. 'What a show we had tonight—wouldn't you say, Arnold?'

'It was a swell 'un all right, Mr Jones!' Lolloping after Wesley was a tall, gangly, wide-eyed young man, whose left leg dragged slightly behind him. Papers spilled out of a folder stuffed under an arm. 'Herbie was powerful spectacular, I thought!'

'Ah, but he always is!' Wesley snatched off the pink top hat. 'Regarding Herbie, I'd pay close attention to Arnold if I were you, folks! He's my stage manager and he's seen the acts a thousand times—why, he might have picked up a few clues about how old Herbie does his tricks!' The pink hat twirled between two thumbs. 'Well, Arnold?'

'I don't know about that, Mr Jones!' The young man rearranged his papers, adjusted his left leg, and stood to attention as best he could. 'Anyways, Herbie'll be down here soon enough! He's just up in his dressing room, taking a rest.'

'Ah—but is he?' Another twirl of the hat, and Wesley winked over its rim. 'Maybe, right at this very moment, he's up there carrying out preparation work for his next *incredible* trick! He never stops, y'know! He works on them endlessly . . .'

Intrigued cooing from the crowd. Harry swung round, and peered up at the rickety theatre building. Seeing brightly lit windows running up the theatre, he had an idea, and began wriggling back between the shoes, trouser legs, boots, and riding-spurs, and nearly collided with Billie and Arthur, who were still only half-way through the crowd.

'Where are you going *now*?' Billie disentangled herself from an umbrella.

'Maybe it'll be easier, Billie!' Arthur was already trying to swivel round. 'Going in the other direction, I mean!'

It wasn't. It was much harder because the crowd was pushing towards the stage door, not away from it, and even Harry needed to wriggle with all his skill before at last he managed to tumble out onto the cobbles. He sprang to his feet, crossed the street and peered back up at the theatre. And he saw exactly what he had hoped for.

In each of the theatre windows, silhouettes flitted of the various performers changing out of their costumes. Two storeys up, neatly framed in its window, was a silhouette that looked recognizably frail. *Herbie*. The old man was moving about, the shadows of his spindly arms fluttering in the light. Spotting a drainpipe running up the side of the theatre, Harry ran across and started shimmying up.

'Harry? What are you doing?'

It was Arthur. He was staggering across the street, his tie wonky, his tweed suit a mess. Behind him, Billie scrambled up from the cobbles with a puzzled expression on her face. They stumbled towards Harry, staring up at the window.

'There's Herbie!'

'I know! I'll climb up and see him. Who knows how long it'll be till he makes it down to the stage door? I know he doesn't want us inside the theatre, but this isn't about tricks any more!' Harry's arm shot up and pointed at various other drainpipes, windowsills, and gutters, a more-or-less possible route up the side of the theatre. 'Come on!'

They didn't look convinced. *Perhaps that's for the best*, thought Harry. A fair number of passers-by were drifting along the street—someone would be sure to notice three children clambering up the side of a theatre, whereas alone, and climbing with skill, he might make the journey undetected. Gripping one of the drainpipe's brackets, he carried on shimmying up through the shadows.

'Harry! Look!'

'What's happening?'

Harry swung round. He saw Billie and Arthur, their arms pointing up at the window. Further down the street, some of the passers-by had stopped and were staring up too. Harry leaned out from the drainpipe, gazed up, and saw why.

The silhouette in the window was no longer just moving about, it was tripping, staggering. Not only that, but someone else seemed to have entered the dressing room. A shadow lurched into view, a thick, burly one, with arms lunging. And whoever it was, it clearly wasn't someone Herbie Lemster was happy to see. The old man's spindly shape was flailing, trying to fend off the shadow, and Harry heard feeble muffled cries, followed by a louder, gruffer shout.

*'What's yours is mine and always shall be! You remember that, Herbie Lemster!'*

A flash of light. Harry's eyes throbbed with pain. An explosion thundered through the night, the drain-pipe shuddered, and he lost his hold. He was falling, the explosion still shuddering as he plummeted down. His arms and legs scrabbled about, thrashing at the air, and he slammed into the sidewalk, his body crumpling.

'Harry?'

He lay there. He felt the sting of the sidewalk's grit cutting deep into his hands, his knees, the side of his head. He lurched to his feet. Stumbling forward, he found a lamp post, and grabbed hold.

'Harry? Are you all right?'

'I'm fine . . .'

It was Billie. Her face peered at him. He saw Arthur coming towards him too. Harry stared at them, blinked, and then swung back to look at the window.

Its glass had been shattered. And corkscrewing out into the night sky . . .

. . . were plumes of thick, purple smoke.

# Chapter 6

Purple wisps drifted down from the window and Harry choked on them, tasting chemicals in his spit. His eyes still throbbed, his body ached from the fall, but he kept stumbling on through the plumes of smog, his gaze fixed on the crowd round the stage door.

'Harry!' Arthur's voice was beside him. 'Did you see it?'

'Whole window blew out!' Billie appeared out of the smoke, flapping at the fumes. 'And look at all this smoke! What the heck's going on, Harry—HARRY?'

*Help Herbie.* Harry plunged into the crowd. It was hysterical now, bodies shoving, legs intertwining. He thought of Herbie's strangely pale face before the show. *And now, a thundering explosion, a shattered window, a load of billowing purple smoke.* The thoughts made him pick up speed, crawling, diving through. Glancing back, he saw his friends, already hopelessly entangled. *They'll catch up.*

'Tell us what happened, Arnold! Speak to me!'

It was Wesley Jones. Harry toppled out between two boots and saw the theatre owner, his pink top hat battered, crouching over the slumped shape of the stage manager. He was trying to sit the gangly young man up on the cobbles, but Arnold's head kept lolling forward, and Harry saw that the stage manager had hit his head, blood trickling all the way down onto his shirt.

'I'd just gone inside, Mr Jones, sir!' Arnold was gasping. 'Herbie was takin' so long, y'see.'

'I know! I sent you!' Wesley swung round to face the crowd. 'You all wanted to see Herbie. I couldn't keep you waiting any longer, could I?'

'So I went in . . . Made my way up the stairs . . .' Arnold choked. 'Then it happened, Mr Jones. The flash of light! The smoke! I lost my balance, see . . . Fell down the stairs . . .'

'And that's where I found him, ladies and gentlemen! At the foot of the stairs!' Wesley butted in. 'He's always a little unsteady on his feet, poor guy! How on earth could he climb the stairs straight into a terrible explosion? To think of such a thing happening, in my theatre of all places—'

'What about the intruder?' someone interrupted. It was one of the passers-by who had watched the window from across the street. 'We saw someone just before the explosion.'

'Intruder?' Arnold's eyes sprang wide. 'What are you talking about?'

'We saw him too!' Another voice from the crowd. 'A shadow, but someone was there all right.'

'He wasn't just there—he was attacking him too! And what about the shout?'

'*What's yours is mine and always shall be!* That's what he said! I heard it, plain!'

'I heard it too!'

'But what does it mean—'

'An intruder in Herbie's dressing room?' Wesley butted in, his face white and wobbling. 'But that makes the business even worse than I thought . . . You see, ladies and gentlemen, I was just about to tell you that . . .' He clutched his pink hat to his chest. 'I managed to find my way to Herbie's dressing room in the end! I stumbled over Arnold here, and climbed the stairs to make sure poor Herbie was all right!' Wesley wailed. 'But there was no sign of him, ladies and gentlemen! No sign at all! Herbie Lemster . . . he's GONE!'

The crowd heaved forward. Harry only just managed to keep himself upright as the surging bodies carried him past Wesley, past Arnold, right into the theatre itself. *A good thing*—maybe he could discover something that would tell him what was going on? He was backstage in the theatre now, surrounded by pieces of scenery, and he lodged himself between one of the enormous seaweed plants from the pearl-diving scene and a collection of ropes and iron hooks, hung on the wall. He watched as the crowd swarmed.

'Intruder? But I saw no one!' It was Bruno the Strongman, still wearing his leopard skin, his muscles shaking. 'I walked up to his dressing room with him after the show, like I do every night—there was no one in there with him then!'

'We didn't see anyone either!' One of the Pearl-Diving Dancers spoke up, surrounded by a tight gaggle of her friends, all in tears. 'We were talking in the corridor! We saw Herbie go into his room and close the door—and that's all! No one visited! The door stayed shut! Until—boom! It knocked us all off our feet!'

'And no one came out of the dressing room after that! I swear it!' The Man Who Told Jokes was still dressed as a parrot, but the face among the feathers was pale and he didn't look like he would said anything funny for quite some time. 'I was at the very far end of the corridor just as it happened! It knocked me back too, but I kept staring at Herbie's door all that time! Sure, it blew open! Sure, there was smoke! But I'd have seen if anyone came out! Particularly if some intruder was tryin' to carry Herbie off against his will! I'd have seen it, I swear . . . '

Harry stumbled towards the nearby stairs. Members of the crowd were racing up them, and he joined them, pushing his way up one flight, then another, and along a corridor until he reached a door on which was painted the letters 'H. Lemster'. He toppled through and saw the shattered windows, some scorch marks on the rug, a few wisps of purple smoke still hanging in the air. But his attention fixed on one item in particular, leaning against the room's solitary chair.

Herbie's walking cane. The stick he had seen in his old friend's trembling hand less than an hour ago.

He started searching. His hands raced over the walls, checking for hidden doors or panels, and he crouched down and inspected the floorboards too. But there was nothing, he was sure of it, not least because everyone else was searching too, countless hands racing over every inch of the room and finding nothing at all. Apart from the door to the corridor, the only other way out was the window, and he himself had been staring at that and would have seen if anyone had tried to get out. What on earth had happened? Harry heard more shouts from outside the room, and stumbled his way back down to the theatre's backstage.

'Poor Herbie! What has become of him!' It was one of the Juggling Acrobats, and she was as upset as all the other performers who had gathered in a sobbing, mournful crowd.

'I'm afraid it's impossible to say!' Wesley Jones wiped at tears with his blood-stained handkerchief. 'Somehow, a mysterious intruder found his way into Herbie's dressing room! An explosion occurred, and the next thing we know both Herbie and the intruder have vanished into thin air!'

'But who was this intruder? What would he want with ol' Herbie?' Arnold wheezed. 'Herbie doesn't have an enemy in the world!'

'Never mind that—how did it happen?' A voice from the crowd, a slightly panicky one. 'How do two men get out of the dressing room without anyone seeing them? Did they just disappear in a puff of smoke?'

'Maybe it was magic!' Another voice, more panicked still. 'Maybe one of Herbie's tricks went wrong? He accidentally summoned this strange intruder and—'

'A demon!' This voice sounded positively hysterical. 'Dark forces! That's what's behind this! Herbie Lemster has been claimed by his own magical powers!'

Pandemonium was breaking out. Harry was about to give up on hearing anything at all, when one voice managed to cut through, louder, more hysterical than any other.

'Magic? Dark forces? I've no idea!' It was Wesley Jones. 'Only one thing is clear, and it's this! Ladies and gentlemen, I regret to confirm to you that . . .' His voice broke with a sob, but kept going. 'Herbert Lemster, marvellous magician, has . . . DISAPPEARED!'

The pandemonium was complete, the screams blotting each other out. It was impossible to hear anything, and it was becoming impossible to see anything either, because the crowd was swarming too fast, too tightly, Wesley and Arnold trying to keep control in the middle. Harry fought his way out. Ducking through the bodies, pushing out through the stage door, he hurried across the street, breathing in the cool night air.

He found a lamp post. He steadied himself against it, his hand gripping the iron. He breathed more deeply. The purple smoke had drifted away, so the air was clear, and its coldness was useful too. Harry stood there, sucking in lungfuls of it as he thought through everything he had discovered about this business so far, and about one piece of information in particular.

*The man he had seen, just a short time ago, as he walked up the theatre's aisle.*

'Harry! What's going on?'

It was Billie and Arthur. Harry saw them racing after him, even as he marched along the street, swung round the corner, and headed towards the theatre's front doors. Had they been backstage in the theatre too, somewhere among the crowd? Or had they been out here the whole time, waiting? Harry lifted an arm, and waved his friends after him.

'Come on! We've got to hurry!'

'Huh?' Billie hurried after him. 'What's happened to Herbie?'

'Tell us!' Arthur cried. 'What did you find out?'

'I've got to check something . . .' Harry slammed through the doors, straight into the deserted foyer. Almost immediately, his friends slammed through after him.

'Check what? Slow down, will you?'

'The man we saw . . . The one with the briefcase . . .' Into the auditorium, and down the aisle. 'Maybe there's some trace of it left behind . . . Some clue . . .'

'Man? Briefcase? What are you talking about?'

'I'll explain everything . . . Just let me . . .'

He turned and stared at a particular seat. He lunged towards it, and his hands explored its back, its arms, the floor around it, searching for anything that might have been left behind. Nothing could be seen, but Harry felt his nostrils twitch as he leaned close to the seat's left arm. He sniffed the arm's worn upholstery. Faintly, very faintly, he could detect the same chemical odour of the purple smoke that had billowed outside.

'Er . . . Harry? What are you doing?'

'Since when did you start sniffing chairs?'

Harry looked up. The expression on Arthur's face was very puzzled indeed, and the corner of Billie's mouth had curved into a smile. Harry stumbled up, straightened his jacket, and pointed back at the chair.

'The man who was sitting right there. He's our only clue.'

And he told them. He told them about those piercing eyes. He told them about the oiled red moustache, and how its ends had curled upwards. As his words raced out, he found himself remembering other details too, the brooch on the cape, the sinister snake coiled around an upright sword, and he told them about those as well. Finally, he told them about the most important, most sinister detail of all.

The man's briefcase.

Out of which had spiralled that tiny wisp of purple smoke.

# Chapter 7

Harry woke up.

He lay there, listening to the sounds of Mrs Mack's boarding house coming to life, the coughs and mutterings of the other lodgers, the scrape of chairs. His nose twitched as he breathed in the smell of Mrs Mack's gruel, which he had long ago learned to avoid. Looking up, he saw beads of morning light sliding through the broken roof tiles over his head, and he lifted his hand, and let the sun play over it, slanting between his fingers, surrounding them. Flexing his fingers, he tried to move them through the criss-crossing rays without them being touched, and succeeded, apart from a single spot of light just glancing his thumb. It was a game he had invented back in the slums of Budapest, his faraway Hungarian home, where the roof over his bed had also been broken. He had played it ever since, and he played it now.

His fingers crept through the light. The smell of the gruel sweetened into the warm fragrance of *zsemle*, the small breads his mother used to make every morning. He breathed it in and heard, very faintly, the whispering of his father, reciting prayers as the family sat by the fire. Harry's fingers crept on, as the sweet smells and whispers drifted around him, and then, all at once, disappeared.

He saw his parents' faces, fearful, tightly drawn. He heard his father's words, but they weren't prayers now, they were frightened mutterings, talk of money and debts, which he hadn't understood back then, and which seemed even murkier as he tried to recall them now. But he had understood what happened next all right. 'The Scattering', they had called it. The family had broken up, his father sending them off across Europe to wherever there might be hope for them, which in his case had meant ending up in the hold of a ship sailing across the Atlantic. Four weeks, the voyage had lasted, four weeks of filth, hunger, and sickness, but even so nothing had prepared him for his arrival in New York, and his new life as a shoeshine boy in this cold, hard city in which he knew no one, no one at all . . .

Harry stared up at his fingers flashing in the light. *These tricks*, he thought, *that was what changed everything.*

Without them, he would still be that shoeshine boy, nothing more. Without them, he would never have met Billie and Arthur, the two best friends he had ever had. Yes, life in New York would be very grim indeed, he thought, if it hadn't been for him picking up these extraordinary skills.

*And that was all thanks to Herbie Lemster.*

Harry sprang up and slid his feet into his boots. A splash of water, and he clattered down the rickety stairs and pushed past the shadows of the other lodgers rising from their beds, labourers, travellers, ne'er-do-wells. Passing a murky mirror by the stairs, he glimpsed himself, and saw various smudges of shoe polish on his face. But there was no time to rub it clean, not this morning.

*Help Herbie.*

He shot out through the rickety front door. Heading off through the Manhattan streets, he swung west to Grand Central Station, where men of business were pouring off the morning trains. Here Harry quickly did a couple of polishing jobs, crouching over the proffered shoes, wiping them clean, shining them up. The cold sidewalk hurt his knees, the polish stung his fingers, but he reminded himself he needed to eat in order to be able to concentrate—today of all days—and so he kept shining until enough coins had dropped into his palm.

Then he hurried to a pastry stall, handed the money over, and stuffed a pie into his mouth. Gathering up any pastry flakes that dangled on his clothes, he ate them too, and walked away from the station, threaded through some alleyways, crossed a market square, slanted along another alley, and arrived at a large hulking factory, grey fumes spooling from it.

Mawkin's Glue Factory, it said on the front. Harry checked a clock in a nearby shop window and ran up to the front door, which was firmly locked. He listened, and made out raised voices on the other side, one deep and growling, the other high-pitched and familiar. *Billie.* The voices grew louder, and something smashed—*time to carry out the plan.* Harry hurried around the back of the factory. Spotting a hay cart on the nearby cobbles, he tugged it across to the factory wall and, with a quick swivel, positioned it correctly. He heard scrabbling sounds from the other side of the wall, and he propped an arm against the cart and tried to look casual in case anyone should pass by, but already something was blurring over the wall's top. The cart wobbled, bits of hay flew, and Billie landed right in front of him, even more spattered with glue than usual. That deep voice bellowed from inside the factory, but, already racing off with his friend down the alleyway, Harry couldn't make out the words.

'Guess that's it for the whole Stirring-Grey-Gloop-For-Two-Cents-An-Hour racket.' Billie tossed her cap into a bin. 'Can't say I mind.'

'You asked him for the day off, I guess?' Harry glanced back.

'Asked him at eight o'clock exactly, just like we agreed. And, obviously, he said no. Not even when I said it was an emergency, which helping poor Herbie most surely is. Said it was his right to make me work the rest of the day, in return for having given me paid work and a bed for so long! And when I told him his pay was nothing and his bed stank of poisonous glue—well, that's when he started chasing me with the broom, so I decided to go for our little plan, and ran for the back wall, tipping a pot of slippery boiled-up bones in his path as I went.' She jerked a thumb back towards the factory, which was already far behind. 'Crummy job.'

'Crummier than all the others?' Harry asked.

'Well now, that's a good question.' Billie slowed down and a frown appeared on her face, just for a few seconds. 'It's true, I've ended up doing a fair few tough jobs on the way up from New Orleans. Cleaning drains, sweeping floors, picking through garbage heaps, you name it.' She peered back again. 'Can't say that was the crummiest boss I've had either, or the first broom I've had to dodge. Still, it's not the sticky situations you get into, it's how you get out of them, that's what I say.' She shrugged, and ducked round a corner. 'Somehow or other, I've managed to get myself unstuck—one way or another. Why, I even managed to get unstuck from a glue factory, didn't I?' Her smile was back. 'Not a bad escape, that. The Glue Pot Scramble, that's what I'll call it. You did well with that cart business too.'

'Thanks, Billie.'

'Sort of makes up for you being so crazy last night.'

Harry felt his face grow warm, even though they were no longer running, just walking along. He looked away, and tried to think of different ways of putting it, but decided in the end just to say what he had said before.

'I'm sorry. I just needed to help Herbie—couldn't think of anything apart from that. And it happens sometimes, you know that. When I—'

'Get swept up in stuff, can't think of anything else, it's how you do your tricks, I know, I know.' Billie speeded up, burst out of the alleyway, and looked about. 'The thing is, this isn't just a trick, is it? It's way more important than that! And we're all friends with Herbie, so we're in this together, yeah?'

'Of course.' Harry's pace quickened.

'Anyway, there's Artie. Come on!'

58

She jumped over some railings and ran across the park. The brilliant white house towered nearby and Harry followed Billie across to the same rhododendron bush as the day before. Waiting behind it stood Artie, his pocket watch ticking in his hand. He looked up at them, jerked his head towards the house, and nodded.

'Thanks, guys. Head over there now. You'll be right on time.'

Harry and Billie set off. They left the park, crossed the street and reached the sidewalk just as the front door of Arthur's house opened. A servant trod down the stone steps. He wasn't as tall as Lord Trilby-Roberts but every bit as stiff, and with a stare every bit as cold. That stare was fixed on the small iron mailbox, a few yards down the sidewalk, and he headed towards it, a collection of letters fluttering in his hand. But he never managed to deliver them, due to the fact that Harry had let himself be pushed by Billie, straight into the servant's path.

'Mind out!'

Harry toppled into the servant. The letters flew everywhere, but Harry snatched them out of the air and, with a swoop of his arm, helpfully posted them into the mailbox.

'Ever so sorry, sir! My friend, she's always doing that . . . Come back here!'

Off he ran after Billie, before the servant could reply. But a flash of his hand had done the trick. As the letters spun in the air, he had spotted the one with a particular address, and it slid into his jacket as the others vanished into the mailbox. It rustled there now, as he followed Billie down the street, back into the park, and behind a tree. They waited until the servant had vanished back into the house, and slid across to the rhododendron bush again.

'Nice work,' Arthur said, taking the letter.

'We just did the snatch.' Harry shrugged, as they walked off. 'How'd you know the servants would be posting the letter to the school at that exact moment?'

'Father gave them instructions yesterday, and they always act immediately. They always post the day's mail at ten o'clock too, and so it stood to reason the letter to the school would be in with it.' He turned, and looked back at the house. 'Father left for Chicago at dawn, by the way. Obviously, he didn't bother to say goodbye.'

His eyes narrowed again. His jaw clenched, and a row of teeth bit down hard on his lower lip. Harry glanced at Billie, worried again. Artie tapped the letter in his hands, swung round, and carried on marching away.

'So what's the next step, Artie?' Billie asked, as they walked out through the park gates, and cut across the street. 'We've got the letter, but how are we going to stop you ending up at this boarding school place? Bad enough, your father acting like you don't exist, but we definitely can't have him sending you 452 miles away—how are me and Harry supposed to cope without our best pal?'

'It's all right, Billie.' Arthur slid the letter into his jacket pocket. 'Now I've got this, it'll all be easy. I've been borrowing books from the library about forgery, copying signatures, that sort of thing. All that research will come in useful now.'

'You're going to write to the school, calling the whole thing off?' wondered Harry.

'Cleverer than that.' Arthur led them round a corner. 'Look, I'll let you know how it goes, but don't worry—I'm staying around.'

'That's good,' said Harry. 'I agree with Billie—we don't want you disappearing anywhere, particularly now there's this stuff with Herbie to sort out.'

'I'm glad you feel that way, Harry,' said Arthur. 'After the way you were last night, I wasn't so sure.'

For the second time, Harry felt his face grow warm. Arthur had turned away, so he couldn't quite see his expression, but his friends were talking about something—he could hear their mutterings, even if he couldn't quite make them out. *Think of something to say, something that will make it better,* he told himself, and he tried to do just that, but it was difficult, and it grew more difficult still, the nearer they came to the destination where they would start work on their vital task. Hadn't Billie herself said, just a few minutes ago, that nothing mattered more than that? Harry thought again of that left-behind walking cane in the dressing room, surrounded by a few wisps of purple smoke.

'It's all right, Harry. I know you didn't mean it.' Arthur tugged his sleeve, and swerved to the left. 'Anyway, it's time to get started.'

Across the street was the New York Public Library. Pillars towered at the top of wide marble steps, and Arthur led Harry and Billie up them, through a pair of bronze doors, and into the huge entrance hall. It dwarfed his tiny tweed-suited figure, but there was something impressive about the speed with which he marched across it, his fingers clicking at his sides, his tie flapping over his shoulder.

'I dropped in here earlier actually, checked a few things, made a good start. But I'm going to need you to draw that moustache again, Harry.'

'No problem, Artie.' Harry followed his friend.

'The snake and sword design too. Maybe you'll remember something else about it this morning? Every detail counts, if we're to find who he is.'

Arthur led them into the reading room, with its high windows and hunched figures scribbling at desks. A swerve to the left, and he pushed through a door. Scampering down a corkscrewing staircase, he led them to the library's musty basement, and started weaving his way through its maze of corridors, each one lined with thousands of books. Fingers still clicking, he didn't hesitate even slightly as he found his way through.

'You sure do know this library well, Artie,' said Harry.

'Certainly spent enough time in here. Remember, before I met you guys, there wasn't exactly much else for me to do.' His voice had gone quiet. Harry peered at him in the gloom, and knew that the quietness was nothing to do with the various signs saying 'Silence', hanging nearby. 'Anyway, who cares about that? We're here.'

'I'll get drawing,' said Harry.

They were at the end of the corridor. A desk stood, covered with carefully stacked piles of books and papers, and Harry immediately sat down at it. Pinned to the wall behind, he saw the various drawings that he had sketched for Arthur the previous night, different attempts at the curling moustache and silver brooch. Immediately, he grabbed a fresh sheet of paper and pencil, and started drawing again. Nearby, Arthur climbed up a wheeled ladder and started leafing through books on a high shelf, and Billie pushed the ladder along, so that he could make his way through them at speed. Harry worked away, trying to remember what he had seen with even more care. Once the drawings were done, he held them up, and Billie was straightaway beside him, snatching them out of his hand, and springing up the ladder with them.

'Useful,' said Arthur, studying the sketches. 'I'm definitely on to something.'

*Clever stuff*, thought Harry, watching his friend tear through books at even greater speed. One thing to be able to spot so many details; another to know what to do with those details. And Billie was hard at work too, leaping up and down that ladder, transporting tottering piles of books back to the desk. Sitting back, Harry gripped the pencil in his fist and wondered if there was anything else he could draw.

The face itself? But that would be much harder than simply drawing a moustache or snake. It would take a highly experienced artist to capture the glimmer of those eyes, the shadowiness of those features, the cruelness of that mouth, all of which had combined to make that face so unsettling. Who was that sinister bulky figure? Harry's grip on the pencil tightened as he thought back to that exact moment, halfway up the aisle, when he had noticed the wisp of smoke and looked up to see that piercing gaze.

'We're only just getting started.' Billie was taking a break, sitting down cross-legged on the table, her boots propped on the edge of Harry's chair. 'It's one thing to work out *who* he is. But then we'll have to figure out *where* he might be—he could be anywhere in New York by now!'

'There'll be a way.' Harry looked up at the blur of tweed-suited arms and fluttering pages, high on the wheeled ladder. 'We just need to let Artie do his stuff.'

'Sure, sure.' Billie's boots swapped places. 'But there's an even bigger thing to figure out—and that's *why*. Some guy breaks into Herbie's dressing room, and makes off with him in a puff of purple smoke— why'd he do that?'

'That's what no one knows.' Harry lifted the pencil to his mouth and gnawed at its end. 'Herbie doesn't have an enemy in the world, they said it over and over again.'

'Doesn't have an enemy in the world that anyone's *heard of.* But if you've got an enemy, you're not likely to go round telling people, are you? Might be safer to keep it quiet.' Billie frowned. 'I've been thinkin' and thinkin', Harry. Did Herbie ever say anything to us that might be some sort of clue? Something about his past?'

'I've been thinking too.' Harry took the pencil from his mouth. 'If only we'd tried to talk to him yesterday. Asked him why he was acting so odd. He'd have let something slip, I'm sure of it.'

'I've got something,' said Arthur, thudding a book onto the desk.

*Gentlemen's Fashion in Eastern Europe.* Harry lifted the cover and flicked through a few pages. Various inked drawings of hats and coats. Not what Harry had expected—but Arthur was already doing the explaining.

'So I started with the moustache. Moustache styles are totally different the world over—as soon as you described this one to me, I knew it wasn't from anyone brought up round here. So I fetched out a whole load of books on fashion and barbering and flicked through. Made a list of likely contenders and, once I'd got your sketch, went for the closest match. Turns out this curled, oiled style is fashionable amongst men in their fifties from Bulgaria, Eastern Europe.' He riffled through the book, and planted a finger on a page. 'Is this the moustache you saw last night?'

There it was, the same moustache, neatly illustrated. *Impressive*—and already Arthur was hurrying back up the ladder, and stumbling down it again with a new pile of books.

'So the fact that he's a Bulgarian doesn't get us very far on its own. But then there's the snake and sword brooch, and that's what I worked on next. It could just be a decoration, obviously. But that's unusual for men—generally, if they wear a brooch or badge, it's because they're part of some sort of organization, and that's the emblem. Now, there are a lot of societies and organizations in the world, but ones with snakes or swords for an emblem, they're rare. Bulgaria narrows it down even more. I'm pretty quick at flicking through books, plus your drawing's dead accurate, Harry, particularly the one you did just now.' Another open book thudded onto the table. 'The badge you saw last night is worn by members of this society, based in Gabrov, Bulgaria.'

Halfway down the page: a snake coiled around a sword. Exactly the same as the one on the lapel the previous night.

'The society's official title is the Grand Gabrov Order of Magical Illusionists.'

*A magician's society.* Harry studied the snake. Its coils were intricate and unfathomable, just like the mystery they were trying to solve. But out of those coils, the snake's head glared clearly, and out of the mystery a single piece of information was glaring at him too. The man in the theatre was a magician. *Makes sense*, thought Harry. Who else would be able to pull off a trick like making an old man disappear from his dressing room in a puff of smoke? *A magician, and a sinister one too.* Those memories flickered again, of Herbie's fear, of those telltale trembling signs. Harry kept staring at the snake, how it curled around the sword. That wisp of smoke had curled too, in a way that was every bit as unnerving. But most unnerving of all had been that face, with its glittering eyes and its long thin nose, long and thin as the blade of a knife—

'Er, Harry?'

Harry looked up. Perhaps his friends were thinking troubling thoughts too. Their eyes were wide open, their faces were even a little pale.

'I think we've discovered something else about that guy you saw, Harry,' whispered Billie, pointing a finger down the corridor.

'What?' Harry turned . . .

'HE'S STANDING RIGHT THERE!'

# Chapter 8

*The sinister magician.* The shadowy shape of the bulky figure could just be seen, framed in the doorway at the corridor's far end. A scrawny library assistant hovered next to him, and that only made him seem more enormous. A black cape swept down from his bulky shoulders, two huge fists hung at his sides, and those eyes glittered in the corridor's gloom. But, so far, he hadn't looked down the corridor. He was too busy, stooped over the librarian, muttering. There was still time.

*No sudden moves.* A panicky leap would cause that huge head to swivel, those eyes to glint. Harry glanced at his friends on either side of him and decided to take no chances. His hands shot out, grabbed Arthur and Billie, and pulled them silently back with a single well-judged step, into the shadows behind them, which were just dark enough to provide cover. *Just like a trick.* Arthur gawped, Billie spluttered as if about to say something and Harry's hands rose again, covering his friends' mouths. He carried on, guiding his friends stealthily back through the shadows, until they reached the doorway at the other end of the corridor.

'Will that be all, Mr Zell?'

So that was his name. The librarian's nervous mutter had drifted through the gloom, and Harry peered back through the doorway. But only by the tiniest amount, because this Zell was moving down the corridor now. Dismissing the librarian with a wave of a hand, the huge magician was striding towards the table at the corridor's side. He reached it, and picked up one of the books that lay there, open at the page with the drawing of the snake and sword. The eyes stared at it, then flicked about the corridor even more keenly.

'What's he doing here?' Billie pushed Harry's hand away.

'It just doesn't make sense!' A muffled hiss from Arthur.

'We only bumped into him for a second, didn't we?'

'So how come he knows we're here?'

'I don't know . . .' whispered Harry. 'I don't . . . WATCH OUT!'

Zell had heard them talking. The huge head snapped round, those eyes glittering straight at the doorway, and Harry grabbed his friends' arms, tugging them off down the corridor so fast that the books on the shelves blurred into one brown smear. Together, they slammed into a spiral staircase, corkscrewed up it, and slanted down another corridor, racing through the gloom.

'He'll head for the main entrance,' Harry gasped. 'That's the obvious way to get out. He'll wait for us there so we need to get out someplace else—any ideas, Artie?'

'Not really, I know the library pretty well, but I've never tried to *escape* from it before—'

'A door that leads outside! A window, anything! There's got to be one!'

'Hang on . . .' Arthur scratched his head as they raced along. 'I think I might have seen some sort of goods entrance, over on the west side—'

'Show us!'

Harry pushed his friend on ahead. Several more corridors, another spiral staircase, endless shelves of books, and they finally arrived at an iron door in the library's west wall. Billie grabbed its handle and pulled.

'Locked!'

'Don't worry!' Harry was already running back along the corridor.

'Don't worry? What do you mean?'

Harry checked the books on the shelves and found one with a couple of notes attached to it by a paper clip. Removing the clip, he ran back to the door, peered through the keyhole, and started bending that little length of wire into a curve.

'Been practising, haven't I. Any bit of stray metal can be a pick, just have to bend it right for the lock.' He gave the clip a final tweak, and slid it in. 'Bent the nail for the padlock yesterday and I had to use my mouth to pick that lock. Using your hands makes it easier and . . .'

A click, a ping, and they were out in the pale September light. A short flight of steps led down to the cobbled street that ran along the library's west side. Harry and his friends toppled down them, their eyes adjusting to the brightness after the library's gloom.

'I just don't get it!' Billie brushed the sleeve of her smock, where Harry had grabbed her. 'How could he possibly know we would be at the library?'

'Maybe he's been following us!' Arthur was straightening his clothes too.

'But why?' spluttered Billie. 'Why would he follow three kids? And how could he have done it? I'd have spotted anyone snooping after me, you bet I would!'

'He's a magician, he can probably do all kinds of things.' Arthur swung round. 'I say, Harry—you don't think he might actually have *real* magic powers, do you?'

'Now *that* would explain it!' gasped Billie. 'There we are investigating him, and he pops up out of nowhere . . . were there any wisps of purple smoke around him just now, Harry? Harry?'

Harry said nothing. His heart was pounding after the run though the library, but his head was pounding too. He lifted his fingers to it. It was as if he could feel the quivering of so many thoughts flying around inside. Zell, that was the magician's name, and he was a member of some kind of magician's society in Bulgaria. But what was he doing here in New York? Why was he so interested in Herbie? How had he managed, magician or not, to make the poor old man vanish from his dressing room, leaving no trace at all—

'THERE HE IS!'

Billie and Arthur were up ahead, peering around the corner of the library. Harry joined them, and peered too. They had been absolutely right not to head for the library's main doors, because Zell was bursting out through them, that bulky head sweeping from side to side as he glanced about. But he clearly couldn't see them, because after a few more glances he strode down the library's marble steps towards a horse-drawn cab wheeling around to meet him. A few muttered words to the driver, and he lurched inside, the whole vehicle tilting with his weight. The driver's whip cracked, the horses' hoofs flung themselves against the cobbles, and the cab rattled off. *Need to be quick*, thought Harry, and he leaped off the kerb, his eyes flicking about as he tried to work out the best way to give chase . . .

'Let's get a cab too.' Arthur pulled open the door of a nearby carriage. 'I'll pay.'

'To the Hotel Crosby, please,' Billie muttered to the driver of the cab that had just pulled up. Arthur jumped inside, and she followed, tugging Harry in after her.

'But . . . the Hotel Crosby? Where's that? How do you know it's where he's going?' Harry bounced around on the seat as their cab rattled away.

'Easy,' said Billie. 'I lip-read what Zell said to the driver, didn't I? Guess I never told you the story of Sherman Jones? The tramp I bumped into when things were truly tough back on the road, Virginia-way? Sherman couldn't hear, but he could lip-read perfectly, and he taught me how to do it too. It's amazing what you can do if you can work out what people are saying without them knowing—explains my brief career as a mind-reader at a fairground.' She laughed. 'We were a good team, me and Sherman. Almost as good as the three of us, right now.' She looked at Arthur and then, quite suddenly, at Harry. 'That was a pretty good stunt we pulled off back there, don't you reckon?'

*Sure was*, thought Harry. And it was going to take many more stunts, every bit as good, if they were going to see this matter through. Three times he had spotted Zell now, and on each occasion he had seemed every bit as threatening. What was this menacing figure's business with poor Herbie? Harry's whole body flinched at the thought. He wound down the cab window and stared out. He saw, down at the far end of a street, Zell's cab wheel to a halt outside a tall, drab building, about ten storeys high. The Hotel Crosby, a sign said. Zell stepped down onto the sidewalk, marched straight up the hotel's steps, and vanished through some revolving doors, a blur of glass and bronze. Harry swung out through the carriage door onto the sidewalk, and peered towards the hotel. He focused in particular on the hotel's doorman, standing right beside the doors, a thick-set fellow wearing a grubby top hat and coat, his arms folded behind his back, his eyes flicking up and down the street in an unfriendly way.

'How are we going to get past *him*?' muttered Arthur, as he and Billie joined Harry. 'Mean-looking fellow.'

'You bet he is,' said Billie. 'But we managed to track Zell down—somehow or other, we'll get into his hotel too. Let's get thinking, Artie.' She started pacing back and forth. 'How about . . . ? What if . . . ?'

'Can I borrow your ukulele, Billie?'

'What?'

It had hit Harry all at once. The plan for getting into the hotel had simply turned up, perfectly thought through. There were risks in it, plenty of them, but nothing he couldn't deal with, and so he decided to put it into action right away. *It's not like Billie's actually come up with a plan of her own yet.* If she had, she would certainly say, he knew that, but instead she was just looking at him in an increasingly baffled way, as he pulled her ukulele off her shoulder and started untuning the strings.

'Harry?'

'A distraction, that's all we need. Just like one of my tricks! If you want people not to see something, you just give them something else to look at—you wave a flower or handkerchief or something and while they're busy looking at that—'

'You're not going in without us, are you?'

It was Arthur who had spoken. Harry looked up, and saw a troubled expression on his friend's face. Next to him, Billie was frowning, her arms crossed.

Harry, still twiddling the ukulele's keys, tried to explain.

'Look, we've got to help Herbie, that's what matters. Remember what we said, Artie—the three of us would never have even met if it hadn't been for Herbie Lemster! Well, he needs our help now—and I think we should give it to him any way we can.'

'That's true.' The look was still on Arthur's face, troubled, and puzzled too. 'It's just that normally, the three of us, we work together. You, me and Billie, we listen to each other, talk things through and—'

'We *will* be working together! We'll just be working on different things, that's all—you'll do the distracting and I'll go in.'

A final twang. The ukulele was out of tune. *They'll come round once they hear the plan properly*, Harry told himself.

And he launched into telling his friends what he needed them to do.

# Chapter 9

Harry hid in the alleyway. The wall behind him was damp, unpleasant smells drifting up from the ground, and a rat crept past one of his boots. But he let none of that distract him. *Just like a trick*—the slightest hesitation or fumble would lead to disaster. *But there won't be any hesitations or fumbles,* he told himself as he peered across the street.

Drifting along it, a discordant twanging. Arthur, looking a bit nervous, was hesitantly strumming the ukulele just outside the Hotel Crosby. Harry had carefully chosen him, not Billie, for the task, and had asked him to attempt one of Billie's most complicated songs too—a ballad about a cowboy trying to cross the Mississippi River—knowing the results would be particularly awful. As for Billie, she was part of the plan as well, and by now she would have taken up her position.

'You stop that din! You stop it now!'

The doorman was shaking his fist. A few of the hotel's guests, as they came down the marble steps, were looking at the tweed-suited, ukulele-twanging boy, one lady even covering her ears, and the doorman had had enough. He was stomping down the steps, his fist still raised, his voice bellowing in Arthur's direction.

'Scram! You hear?'

Arthur scrammed. He ran as fast as he could, but the doorman was nearly upon him, and he would easily have grabbed him if the garbage can by the nearby railings hadn't toppled forward. *Perfect.* Crouched behind the metal can, Billie had done her bit, kicking it forward at just the right time, and the doorman had stumbled straight into it, his fist flailing after the fleeing Arthur. He didn't even see Billie as she darted away from the railing in the opposite direction.

*And he definitely won't see me,* thought Harry as he flew up the marble steps and slid through the revolving doors. As they spun around him, he peered through, made out what he needed, and decided his next move. Stepping out into the lobby, he lunged sideways. A couple of porters pushed a luggage trolley, a clerk was working at the reception counter, but no one saw him because he was safely behind the large aspidistra plant to the left of the doors. Not one of the plant's leaves was even slightly trembling—*nicely done.* The clerk stood up from the counter and was wandering off across the lobby towards a pair of double doors as Harry slid out from the aspidistra, hurried across the hall, and glided behind the counter. Grabbing the hotel guestbook, he bundled himself into a cupboard.

He pulled the door almost shut, leaving a tiny shaft of light to spill on to the pages as he turned them. The names of all the hotel's guests were written on them, along with their room numbers and the date they had signed in. His finger slid down the list but he didn't recognize any names. Then his finger stopped, halfway down the ledger's second page.

'Boris Zell. Arrived 14th September. Room 760.'

So there he was. Boris Zell, that was his full name. Boris Zell, who was a member of the Grand Gabrov Order of Magical Illusionists. Boris Zell, who had been seen at the theatre clutching a briefcase from which that telltale wisp of purple smoke curled. Boris Zell, who had uncannily turned up at the library just now—so uncannily that Arthur and Billie, with some fairness, had put it down to actual magical powers. Harry closed the ledger, slid out of the cupboard and rummaged about the counter, searching for any possible clue about the guest in Room 760.

His hands flew about, finding nothing. But there was a door just along from the counter on which was written 'Manager's Office', so he decided to try that. He pushed at the handle and found it was locked. *Another pick*—and his spare hand was already reaching back to the counter, towards something he had spotted, a dirty fork and plate, the remains of the reception clerk's breakfast. *Perfect.* Harry grabbed the fork, wiped it on his sleeve, bent back three of its prongs, peered into the lock's keyhole, and curved the fourth prong until it was exactly the right shape. He pushed the prong into the keyhole, angled it upwards and . . .

The lock sprang open. Harry bent back the prongs and replaced the fork neatly on the plate. Then he slid into the manager's office and noticed, right away, the day's post, a knotted bundle on the manager's desk. He undid it, riffled through the letters. Two of them were for Mr Boris Zell, both in Bulgarian, which Harry didn't understand, so he tossed them aside. But filed with them was a telegram in English, addressed to Boris too. Harry lifted it up, and read it carefully.

TO: MR. BORIS ZELL C/O HOTEL CROSBY, NY.
FROM: MR. OSCAR MUNTZ, MANAGER, VARIETY THEATRE,
CHICAGO.
    WE CONFIRM BOOKING OF YOUR ACT FOR EVENING
1ST OCTOBER 1886. WE NOTE YOU CLAIM YOUR ACT WILL
CONTAIN CERTAIN NEW TRICKS, ENTITLED: BICYCLING
OVER SPIKES, THE FLYING KNIVES, AND SPIDER UP
SLEEVE. WE WILL ADVERTISE SUCH TRICKS AND THERE-
FORE INSIST YOU PERFORM THEM OR NO FEE PAYABLE.

Just a single sheet of paper that would have cost twenty cents to send, no more. But this was without question a very important discovery, and an unsettling one too. Harry dropped into a nearby chair to take it all in. *Why would anyone want to make off with poor Herbie in the first place?* Here, resting in his hand, was a possible, and very unpleasant, answer to Billie's question.

The Game, that was what Herbie had called it. Magicians studied other magicians, seeking to uncover the secrets to each other's tricks. It had been going on for more than a thousand years, Herbie had said. But what if one magician chose to take the Game a little bit too far? What if a magician tried to get hold of the secret to some tricks, not simply by watching— but by any means he could?

'Poor Herbie,' Harry muttered.

The telegram proved it. It was clearly a reply to one Boris had sent earlier, seeking a booking for his show. Nothing wrong with that—except for the list of acts Boris was offering. They were Herbie's tricks. 'Bicycling Over Spikes' must refer to the one in which Herbie floated effortlessly over the bed of spikes as if riding a bicycle, and 'The Flying Knives' and 'Spider Up Sleeve' were Herbie's too. Boris was promising to perform Herbie's tricks—yet how could he do that if he didn't know their secrets? So that was the telegram. But what about the shout that had been heard that night?

*'What's yours is mine and I shall have it!'*

Herbie hadn't just disappeared. He had been kid-napped. Boris had snatched him from his dressing room—and if he was ruthless enough to do that, what might he be doing now? Would he have imprisoned Herbie somewhere, starving him until he gave up what he knew? Or did he have other devices, as mysterious and sinister as his purple smoke, with which he could persuade the old man to blurt out his dearly kept secrets . . . ?

The office door was opening. Sunk in the chair, Harry had almost forgotten where he was. Stuffing the telegram into his pocket, he leaped up and rolled under the desk as the hotel manager, a short, bustling man, rushed in. Fortunately, he left the door open behind him, so Harry was able to slide out to the safety of the reception counter. *I'll break into Room 760*, he decided—in there, he would discover clues to how Boris had performed this kidnapping, where he might have hidden poor Herbie, and more besides. But for now, he just needed to get out from behind this counter. Peering over it, he made out the porters and some guests, but no one was looking directly towards him, so he made a dash for it, sliding across the marble floor towards the aspidistra. *Perfectly timed*, he thought, and then he saw something, and realized he was much, much too late.

A bulky figure was striding across the lobby. A dark cape swept down to his shoes, a dark hat tipped over his face. The figure stopped, and looked straight at Harry, who was still several feet away from the plant.

It was Boris Zell.

# Chapter 10

Those cruel eyes glittered. A lip flexed and, above it, the oiled moustache curled. On the dark cape, the snake-and-sword brooch gleamed. Worst of all, as Harry skidded towards the aspidistra, the telegram rustled in his pocket, evidence of Boris Zell's utterly ruthless plan.

*Ruthless regarding Herbie*, he thought. *And probably just as bad for anyone who tried to help him.*

'You! You were there . . .' Those piercing eyes narrowed. 'Last night at the theatre . . . I saw you!'

The face darkened. Nostrils flared. Harry decided not to hang about. Besides, the bustling hotel manager had just slammed out of his office, and was pointing a finger straight at Harry.

'He's been in my office! Gone through the post and everything! Stolen something too, I'd say! Catch him quick!'

Harry dived past Zell. He tried to reach the revolving doors but found himself staring at the doorman, who was marching back in. He struck off across the lobby instead, but everywhere he looked, porters, clerks, and even some of the guests were running towards him. He threw himself through a pair of double doors. His boots pounded down a corridor, voices bellowing behind him.

'Stop him!'

'Thief!'

His boots pounded on, and his heart pounded even faster. On he raced, towards some double doors. He risked a glance behind him—his pursuers were getting closer. He slammed through the doors. Darting to the left, he burst onto a stairwell and raced up three flights of stairs, his pursuers' cries spiralling up after him.

'We've got him now!'

'Block off the other staircase!'

'He can't keep going up for ever!'

More doors. Another corridor, on the hotel's third floor. Windows ran along one side of it and, as Harry flashed past them, he turned his neck so that he could study their shiny brass fastenings. Down by his side, his fingers fluttered, rehearsing the lightning-quick action he would need. Up ahead, he saw that the corridor turned. *It might work, it just might* . . . Racing round the corner, he glanced back. He could hear his pursuers' stampeding boots, but they hadn't reached the corner, not yet. His arm flung towards a window, his fingers threw the fastening at lightning-speed and . . .

He climbed out through the open window and shimmied along the sill. Harry reached the end and, grabbing a drainpipe, pushed the window shut behind him with his left boot. On one leg, he balanced at the sill's end, out of view. Muffled by the glass, he heard his pursuers' boots thud past.

'Faster! He's only a boy!'

'Catch him!'

*The Hotel Crosby Disappearing Act.* As far as the hotel porters were concerned, he would have completely vanished, leaving no evidence at all—who would be keen-eyed enough to notice that the latch of a single window wasn't fastened? *But the trick's not all done yet.* Balancing at the edge of a third-floor windowsill, he knew it was only a matter of time before someone looked up and spotted him. He needed to get down and, staring at the street below, he saw a way.

He waited, watching, calculating the right moment. Then he let go of the drainpipe, stepped off the sill, and plummeted thirty feet into a garbage cart trundling along the street.

Harry crashed, deep into the garbage. Potato peelings, soggy newspaper, the remains of meals slithered around him. Gagging, he gripped the edge of the cart and swung himself out onto the cobbles, trying to ignore the slime leaking out of his shoes and the shouts of the driver as the cart trundled away. He ignored the potato peelings on his jacket too, and the sludge dripping from his hair, as he stumbled off down the alleyway, slanting left, weaving right until the Hotel Crosby was far behind. Stopping by a water pump, he worked the handle up and down, rinsing himself off. Then he hurried on through more alleyways, more streets, until he arrived at the particular sidewalk corner where, as had been agreed, his friends were waiting.

'Billie? Arthur? It's me!'

They didn't look up. They seemed deep in a conversation about something. Billie was talking at speed, waving her hands in the air, and Arthur was busily making notes on a little pad. *What are they doing?* Harry walked right up to Billie, and tugged her sleeve.

'The plan worked great—thanks, you two.' Harry knelt and picked up his shoeshine box, which Billie had safely kept for him. 'Boris Zell, that's his full name, and he's staying in Room 760. And I found something else out too—it's serious.'

Something was up with them. Billie had crossed

her arms again, and Arthur was avoiding his eye. But, at the same time, they couldn't help being interested in what he was saying, and they started looking even more interested, the more the story flew out of him, and particularly when he tugged the telegram from his pocket.

'So he's been kidnapped?' Arthur pored over it. 'But that's terrible!'

'I'm trying to think of another explanation, Artie.' Billie inspected the paper, and handed it back to Harry. 'But what Harry says adds up, unfortunately.'

'We should tell the police.' Arthur frowned. 'Herbie could be in real danger—'

'It's not that easy!' Harry had already thought this through. 'Who's going to believe us? Three kids, and all we've got is this telegram. They're not going to arrest Zell just because of that. The most they'll do is ask him a few questions, and then he'll know he's in danger and he'll check out of the Hotel Crosby and vanish, simple as that. How are we going to help Herbie then? No, we need to get into his room and get more proof. Then the police will have to believe us.'

He watched his friends. After a while, the two of them nodded, although Billie also wrinkled her nose.

'What's that smell?' Her eyes fixed on a potato peeling, still on Harry's sleeve.

'I noticed it too.' Trying to hide a smile, Arthur took a couple of steps back from Harry. 'Pretty nasty.'

'It doesn't matter.' Harry brushed the peeling off. 'I was just getting to that bit, when I had to make a run for it and—'

'You got seen?' Billie looked straight at him. 'Right—we're definitely taking charge now!'

'What? Why?'

'You can't go back in there again! Doesn't matter if you walk, sneak, or crawl, they'll be looking out for you.'

'She's right, Harry.' Arthur shrugged. 'If they saw you, they'll know your face. You'll never get in, distraction or no distraction—'

'Course I'm right!' Billie was pacing. 'The Atlantic City Laundry Caper, Artie! That settles it!'

The Atlantic City Laundry Caper. What was she talking about? *No time for Billie's stories*, thought Harry, spinning round. Apart from anything else, he was too busy thinking about something else Billie had said. She was right—it was going to be very hard to get back into the Hotel Crosby now he had been seen—and that was extremely serious, as far as their plan was concerned. Harry ran across the street and hopped onto a fire hydrant, nibbling a fingernail as he did so. For Herbie's sake, he had to get back in—but how? He peered up at the tall dark shape of the hotel, a few streets away. Together with the buildings around it, it loomed high in the air . . .

*High in the air.*

'Harry?' Arthur's voice, strangely wobbly, called after him. 'What are you doing?'

Harry stood on the fire hydrant, perfectly balanced. The plan to rescue Herbie, that was what mattered and, in the nick of time, he had thought up the next bit of it. Not only that, but he knew where he would be able to get his hands on the bits and pieces of equipment he needed. Not only *that*, but he had spotted, trundling towards him, gathering speed, a streetcar with the number 47 chalked on its front. He extended an arm.

'Harry!' It was Arthur again. 'Why won't you listen to us! Why won't you—'

The streetcar swept past and Harry flew off the hydrant. Streetcar Number 47 would take him where he needed to go, and it wasn't hard to hold on, not after all the practice he had put into the trick of his, crossing Sixth Avenue by leaping between streetcars just like this one. *More than just a trick now*, he thought, as he clung to the streetcar's side, ducking to avoid a shower of sparks. He swung round, trying to see his friends.

They were standing there, down the street. That troubled, puzzled look was back on Artie's face. Billie, stood next to him, looked a little fiercer, but she also had an arm round Artie for some reason. Harry stared, and tried to make them out more clearly.

But sparks kept showering, making it impossible to see. And by the time the glittering flare had cleared, the streetcar had swerved around the corner.

His friends were nowhere to be seen.

# Chapter 11

Harry leaped off the streetcar and landed on the sidewalk. The ride across Manhattan had blown most of the garbage smell out of his clothes, but he checked himself in a nearby grocer's window anyway and flicked a final potato peeling from behind his ear. Then he headed for the Wesley Jones Theatre, his shoeshine box clutched under his arm.

Equipment. That was why he had come to this place, but it was a useful opportunity to find out a bit of useful information too. After all, this was the very theatre where Herbie's kidnapping had taken place. Swinging his shoeshine box off his shoulder, Harry set it up by the stage door, and waited for the theatre folk to drift in from the surrounding streets, Bruno the Strongman, the Pearl-Diving Ladies, the Cossack Dancers. Then he noticed someone standing next to him. It was Arnold, the gangly, wide-eyed stage manager with the weak left leg.

'Shoeshine, sir?' Harry peered up. 'Just four cents, that's half-price. It'd be an honour, sir, to shine the shoes of someone who works at the Wesley Jones Theatre—it's my favourite theatre in New York, sir.'

A nice bit of patter. He could generally rely on getting himself a job, and the patter seemed to have done the trick on Arnold, although he didn't seem very happy about it. Sadly, the stage manager lifted his good leg and dumped the shoe on the end of it onto Harry's box.

'Yeah, I'll have a shoeshine.' Arnold sighed. 'Anything to make things look better on a day like today! D'you hear what happened here last night, shoeshine boy?'

'I did, sir.' Harry rubbed in a blob of polish. 'Poor Herbie Lemster . . .'

'Of course you've heard of it! All New York's talking about it!' Arnold rubbed at his eyes. 'A mystery, that's what they're saying. But it's more than a mystery to us. It's a catastrophe! The most awful thing that's taken place at this theatre! How could it happen? To one of our very own, shoeshine boy?'

What a state he was in. The bruise he had suffered falling down the stairs was still on his forehead, dark and sore-looking, but that was nothing compared to the sadness of his expression. His large eyes shone with tears, one of which splashed down on the shoe

Harry was polishing, messing up the shine. Harry wiped it away, and re-polished the leather. Then he heard another voice and, looking round, he saw a face that was gloomier still.

'Terrible! Just terrible!'

It was Wesley Jones. The theatre owner had just stumbled out of a horse-drawn cab. His pink hat was battered, his clothes were crumpled, and it was as if his plump body had crumpled too, his face sagging, dark bags under his eyes, his skin drained to a sickly white. He glanced at Harry, but hardly seemed to take him in as he carried on talking to his stage manager.

'What can have become of him, Arnold? I haven't been able to sleep all night!'

'No one knows nothin', Mr Jones.' Arnold shook his head, and pointed down at Harry. 'You should treat yourself to a shoeshine too, Mr Jones. This boy charges just four cents. Might cheer you up?'

'Nothing could do that!' Wesley Jones tugged out a handkerchief and dabbed his eyes. 'Still, only four cents, you say? To do my shoes?'

'Sure.' Harry finished Arnold's toecaps with a flourish.

'Done. Come on up to my office and do my shoes, then.' Wesley tossed Harry four cents, turned, and trod sadly into the theatre. 'All twenty pairs of them.'

*Twenty pairs? All for just four cents?* Still, at least he had been invited into the theatre. Harry's eyes flicked about as Wesley Jones led him through the gloomy backstage area, up a rickety staircase, along various corridors. What a ramshackle building it was. In particular, the plumbing seemed completely chaotic, countless pipes winding along the walls, taps and dials jutting off them. Everywhere he looked, he could see pipes, many of them wobbling with the sheer pressure of the water inside, a few even sprouting leaks, but he reminded himself that he was hardly here to carry out a plumbing check. *Polish Wesley's shoes, perhaps do a bit more chatting, and slink off for the equipment.* Harry followed Wesley all the way to his office, a surprisingly well-kept room with wallpaper that more or less clung to the wall, a plush rug, and a mantelpiece with various framed photographs on it. And, of course, there were Wesley's shoes, a whole rack of them in a cupboard. The theatre owner collapsed into a chair by the desk, and Harry started work, unscrewing polish cans, fluttering cloths, and plunging into the conversation.

'So, hasn't anyone discovered *anything* about—'

'About poor Herbie? Nothing at all!' Wesley sank even further into his chair, his arms trailing over the sides. 'The police were here late into the night!

Detectives too. They worked the whole building over, bottom to top. But they ain't discovered a thing!' His face sagged, its eyes wet and mournful. 'People say it's a trick gone wrong. They say it's dark forces! They say it's all kind of stuff. But what have they actually found out? Nothing!'

'Nothing, Mr Jones?' Harry kept polishing.

'Not a darn thing!' One of Wesley's hands pounded the arm of his chair, the other fluttered a handkerchief over his face, collecting the tears from his eyes. 'All we got is one thundering explosion, one storm of purple smoke, an intruder that no one properly saw, and some yelled-out words that no one understands! It's terrible, shoeshine boy! Just terrible!'

*No information whatsoever.* Harry tried to make out his reflection in the shoe he was polishing which, for some reason, remained murky no matter how hard he rubbed. Perhaps he should tell Wesley what *he* knew? The distressed theatre owner would almost certainly want to hear Harry's discovery about Herbie being kidnapped for his tricks—wouldn't he? *Possibly*, thought Harry, polishing on. But, like the police, the theatre owner was hardly going to take the word of a kid, particularly not a scruffy shoeshine boy reduced to cleaning twenty pairs of shoes for four cents. Like the police, at best he could probably just make a few inquiries at the Hotel Crosby, and that would only alert Zell with disastrous results . . .

'What do you think, Arnold?' Wesley swung towards the office door, through which the stage manager had pushed, his left leg dragging behind him. In his hands he carried a tray with a teapot and cups on it, along with, curiously, a leather bag with a spanner protruding from it. 'Who could be behind this horrible deed? Who'd want to do harm to Herbie? He hadn't an enemy in the world, surely?'

'Absolutely not, Mr Jones! I never heard of no one not liking the guy, and I can't imagine it, neither. He really was one gentle fella . . .'

The tea tray rattled in Arnold's wobbly grip, and he nearly dropped it, the leather bag slithering out of his grasp too, and it was up to Harry, lightning quick, to leap across the rug and catch the teapot, the cups and the saucers before they hit the rug, and he just managed to grab the bag too, which he saw was full of all kinds of spanners, wrenches and other tools. Meanwhile, Wesley rose from his chair, and lowered the unsteady Arnold into it in his place.

'Forgive my stage manager! He was so very fond of poor Herbie! Mind you, you're fond of all our fine company, aren't you Arnold?' He nodded down at his stage manager's weakened leg. 'He used to be a performer himself, a trapeze artist, until his unfortunate injury! So he knows how delicate performers can be, how carefully they must be looked after. You attend to their every need, do you not, Arnold?'

'That I do, Mr Jones.' Arnold lifted a feeble hand towards the bag of tools, which Harry gave him. 'Was just about to do that plumbing job, sir.'

'Ah yes, the plumbing!' Wesley flung an arm at one of the theatre's many wobbling pipes which snaked across the office's ceiling. 'We are attempting to install running water in each and every performer's dressing room. But we prize our performers, and so no effort shall be spared on their behalf. And none of them are prized more greatly than . . .'

'Than poor Herbie Lemster!' Arnold stared at the rug.

'Indeed!' Wesley tottered to the mantelpiece, and the row of framed photographs which, Harry could now see, were of the theatre's performers, Bruno the Strongman, the Juggling Acrobats, and the rest. 'Why, I count him as one of my dearest friends. He has worked happily at this theatre for no less than ten years.' He grabbed one of the framed photographs and held it aloft. Staring out of it, Herbie's face, wan and wrinkled. 'He just did occasional appearances for me at first but, as our acquaintance grew, he did more and more until in the end he asked to become one of my regular acts, performing every night at the theatre that I am proud to say he considers his true home!'

'His home, nice and cosy.' Arnold sadly contemplated a spanner.

'Yet it is his home no longer. Because he has disappeared! DISAPPEARED!' Wesley held up the photograph frame, looked at Harry, and looked back at the picture again. 'I say, I don't suppose you polish picture frames do you?'

Harry had only just finished the shoes. He was about to protest that he had no silver polish, but Wesley had already fetched a small can out of a drawer, and tossed it at him. For the next ten minutes, Harry polished the frame, the odd green polish making his skin itch; Herbie's face staring up at him, wrinkled, mysterious, offering no help whatsoever. *But the mystery will be solved*, Harry decided, placing the photograph back on the mantelpiece.

He made his way down through the theatre. Wesley and Arnold had left him alone to do the polishing task, and Harry knew it would be easy to slink off unnoticed, but he decided to visit the other performers. *Maybe they'll be more helpful.* Visiting their dressing rooms, he offered to shine their shoes, and tried to ask a few questions. In the corner of each room, a sink gurgled mournfully, the result of Arnold's plumbing work, Harry deduced.

Not a scrap, not a snippet. The performers had no information for him at all. Still quivering with the shock of what had happened, they would be in an even worse state if they knew Herbie's possible fate, that he was probably being held captive by Boris Zell and forced to give up his tricks. *Good thing I'm on the case,* thought Harry, as he slid out of the final dressing room and headed off towards his main task, the gathering of equipment. Creeping down to the murky backstage area he sought out the exact place where he had sheltered the previous night after being swept in with the crowd. The wooden seaweed stood there, but he also made out several coils of rope hanging on the nearby wall, some with iron hooks on the end. *Perfect.* Harry chose the best rope, over forty foot long, along with a medium-sized hook, and stuffed them under his jacket.

'Lost, shoeshine boy?'

It was Arnold. He was staring at Harry from a little way off in the backstage gloom. Harry wriggled and the bulge in his jacket slid round the back. He walked towards the stage manager, his shoeshine box swinging from his hand.

'Took a wrong turn, couldn't see where I was going.'

It was believable enough, it was very dark. 'Sorry about that, Mr Stage Manager.'

Arnold said nothing. Wrapped up in mournful thoughts about Herbie, he was clearly having more troubles with the theatre's plumbing too, his shirt-sleeves soaked with water, spanners clutched in his hand. Silently, the limping figure led Harry to the stage door. Harry hurried out, and he must have accidentally knocked the stage manager off-balance, because Arnold swayed, and steadied himself by gripping Harry's shoulder with a surprisingly fast, strong hand.

'Thanks for dropping by, shoeshine boy.'

Another wobble. But Arnold steadied himself, and the hand let go. Harry offered up a smile, and hurried away from the theatre.

The coil of rope and the hook were tucked neatly inside his jacket.

# Chapter 12

Harry stopped off at the West Side docks, a favourite spot for practising his tricks, quiet apart from the lapping of the Hudson and the horns of passing ships. Among the warehouses and cranes, he spent nearly half an hour with the rope and hook, swinging them, spinning them, sending them flying. The trick was hard in all sorts of ways, and the way it needed to be set up was no exception. Patiently, he perfected the throw, judging the flick of his wrist, jerking back his arm at exactly the right moment and, by the time it worked, his arms and fingers ached from the practice. *Herbie's depending on it*, he thought, and the pain vanished, as he ran off, weaving through the crowds, cabs and horses at double speed, back towards the looming Hotel Crosby.

Billie and Arthur were right—there was no way on earth he could walk, sneak, or crawl back into that hotel. But walking, sneaking, crawling wasn't what he had in mind. Tall though the drab hotel was, even taller buildings stood nearby, including the one across the street from it, an office block of some kind. A fire escape ran up that building's side, its rickety iron girders no more than twenty feet away from the hotel. Fixing his gaze on a spot about two-thirds of the way up the fire escape, Harry walked even faster, the coiled rope and hook dangling from his hand.

'Harry? Where have you been?'

It was Arthur, running towards him through the crowd. He had a slightly unusual look to him, his tie sticking out, his hair in a mess, his face flushed pink. *What's he been doing?* Looking around, Harry saw no sign of Billie, and wondered what she was doing too, but then spotted a clock over a nearby shop, and knew there was no time for that. It had been nearly two hours since he had last been at the hotel, and Boris Zell could have been getting up to all manner of things—it was time to begin.

'I've been practising, Artie!' He held up the rope. 'Look!'

*Odd.* Usually, Arthur reacted to news of a new trick with interest, his eyes widening, sometimes his mouth falling wide-open too. But that wasn't happening now. He just blinked at the rope, his face turning a little pinker, even red. *Maybe I just need to explain it a bit more,*

Harry thought, as he sprang towards the fire escape that ran up the side of the building near the hotel.

'Harry!' Arthur called after him. 'Wait! I've got something to tell you . . . Me and Billie, we've . . .'

'Everyone at the Hotel Crosby will be looking for me, Artie.' Harry clanged up the iron stairs. 'But that doesn't mean they'll be looking UP—true?'

'Looking up? What do you mean?'

Harry sprinted on upwards, nearly ten storeys, until he was level with the Hotel Crosby's roof. Pulling the rope off his shoulder, he twirled it, narrowed his eyes, and threw it. His arm ached from the practice, but it had definitely been worth it, because the hook at the rope's end soared neatly across the twenty-foot gap. It clanged against the railing that ran round the Hotel Crosby roof, looped around, and caught hold. Harry hauled at the rope until it was iron-tight. *Artie'll understand the trick now.* From further down the fire escape, he heard footsteps, and he turned to greet his even more red-faced friend, who was struggling up the last flight of steps towards him.

'The tightrope trick! Remember? Billie strung the rope between two trees! I walked across it, and wriggled my hands free of twenty-five knots at the same time?'

'Harry . . . Listen . . .' Arthur was out of breath. 'Please, I . . .'

'If I can walk a tightrope while doing that, I can easily walk one with my hands free! I know it's higher up, but as long as I stay on the rope who cares how high it is?' Harry tore off his boots, tied the laces, and hung them round his neck. His bare feet flexed, ready for the walk. 'So once I'm across, I just jump onto the roof, and get into the hotel from there—'

'Harry!' Arthur had reached the fire escape landing and seen the taut rope. His face turned redder still, and he spluttered the words breathlessly out. 'Why aren't you listening to me? We're a team, remember? Me, Billie and—'

'I know we're a team! Just let me finish, Artie! So I go down into Room 760 and get in. I discover everything I can, then I run back up to the roof. I just need you to guard the rope, Artie—Artie?'

He had explained it all pretty clearly. Yes, he had been talking very fast, but surely the trick was plain to see. Particularly when he was actually balanced on the railing, one foot on the rope, the breeze from the street curling up around him. But Arthur still wasn't reacting in the usual way. He was just standing there, staring at the rope, that troubled look on his reddened face. Then he swung round, stomped over to the other side of the fire escape, and peered down. *Makes no sense at all*, thought Harry.

UNLESS . . .

'Where's Billie?'

'At last! Paying attention to me! There she is— down there!'

'What?'

'If you'd only listened you'd already know. You see, you don't need to break into the hotel.'

'Don't need to?' Harry looked down at the quivering rope. 'But I'm almost there already . . .'

'So's Billie.' Arthur shot an arm down at the street. 'Look—right down there!'

Harry jumped down and leaped across the fire escape. And it was, he had to admit it, pretty astonishing.

Billie was walking up the hotel's front steps. But he wouldn't have recognized her if she hadn't been pointed out. An elegant silk gown swept down from her shoulders, peacock feathers sprouted from a bonnet and, most impressively, a large pair of wire-framed dark-lensed spectacles wobbled on her nose, giving her a mysterious air. She was also several inches taller, and Harry glimpsed, just under the hem of the silk dress, some wooden blocks attached to the bottom of her boots. No wonder she was swaying slightly, as she twirled a dainty umbrella, and headed up towards those revolving hotel doors.

'Wha—What is she doing, Artie?'

'It's all based on the Atlantic City Laundry Caper.'

'The what?' Vaguely, he remembered the words. 'But—'

'It's a pretty simple business, really. I think you're going to like it, now you're actually listening,' said Arthur, swinging round. He put an arm round Harry, and a smile was back on his face. 'So, back on the road, Billie rolled up in Atlantic City, right out of cash. She needed to get a job quick, so she tried to get one at a laundry, a fancy one for ladies and gents and their fancy clothes. The owner said she'd have to prove herself by washing a load of his stinky stockings and shirts, which she did, and did it perfectly too. But the owner didn't give her the job and didn't pay her for the socks and shirts either! Just rolled around laughing, saying he'd never in a month of Sundays have a "dirty hobo kid from New Orleans" messing up his fancy clean laundry! Big mistake. Billie grabbed a few bits and pieces off a laundry line, and disguised herself as the servant of some rich lady who'd just arrived in town and—'

'But . . . How . . .' Harry tried to take it all in.

'I'm getting to that! She stuck blocks of wood under her shoes to make herself taller, pulled a bonnet over her face, and counted on the thick laundry steam to stop anyone looking too closely. Clever, eh?' Arthur chuckled. 'She just turned up at the door, asked the maids who worked there about placing a large order on behalf of her mistress for washing household linen and, while they were fetching the owner, she slipped in, vanished into the steam and tipped seventeen boxes of washing powder into one of the vats. Bubbles everywhere. That owner got himself a fancy clean laundry all right—took nearly two days to rinse the place through! Pretty good, don't you think?' Arthur pointed back down at the hotel steps. 'And it's come in pretty handy for this Herbie business too, I'd say.'

Billie was at the top of the steps now, bulked-up shoes, silk dress and all. She was mumbling to the doorman, making various grand gestures with the umbrella. And whatever she was saying, it seemed to work, because the doorman stood aside, and the elaborately disguised street girl swept through the revolving doors. The doors spun behind her and Arthur, with a small, precise action, nodded.

'But this disguise—I don't see how it works.' Harry stared at the still-spinning doors. 'One thing to pretend to be a servant—but what's she pretending to be now?'

'That's mainly down to me.' Another tweak of his tie. 'I remembered reading that particular hotels are often popular with particular professions—word spreads, you see. So I asked myself—if this Boris Zell uses the Hotel Crosby, maybe other magicians do too? I ran back to the library, and did some research, checked through old newspapers and hotel guides— and it turns out I was right. Magicians, illusionists, men of the theatre—they've been using the Crosby for years. So would they be surprised if someone a bit exotic and theatrically dressed turned up—I don't think so.' He was speaking quickly now. 'The more exotic the better, probably. Billie and I had a quick think and, with the help of a few more books, we invented a whole new magician for her to be—Princess Moldo, that's who she's going to check in as!'

'Princess Moldo?' Harry had no idea what to say.

'The famous illusionist from Peru. I've been running around like mad ever since, finding out a few other things, buying the bits of costume, the dress, the umbrella—and not forgetting those dark spectacles.' He pointed back down towards where Billie had been, wearing those glittering frames. 'Do you know they actually come from Peru? From Lima? Found them in an antique shop—the Princess Moldo Spectacles, I'm calling them—'

'But—costume, spectacles, umbrellas—it must have cost a fortune . . .' Harry butted in.

'A fair bit, yes, but my allowance covered it.' Arthur tapped his wallet, inside his jacket. 'What else am I going to spend my money on, apart from my friends? Us and our plans, Harry, that's all that matters.' Briefly, that troubled look returned. 'To me, anyway . . .'

*It might just work.* Harry was still taking in a lot of what Arthur had said, but it was clear that this scheme was a good one, and so far it had worked too. But would it continue to succeed? Getting through the door disguised as a Peruvian illusionist princess was clever, there was no question about that. But how exactly was Billie going to break into room 760 itself? What about checking in at the hotel reception, which would need forms to be filled in, questions to be answered, during which time her disguise could easily be detected? All risky . . .

'Harry? What are you doing?'

'I'm going in too.' Harry was back on the rail. 'Like I said, I'm almost there anyway.'

'But Billie and me . . . We're the ones who are doing this!'

'Why can't we carry out my plan too?' One foot edged out on the rope. 'Doubles our chances, just in case something goes wrong. Herbie's been kidnapped, Artie! Zell could be doing all sorts of stuff to him, and he won't stop until he gets the secret to his tricks and—'

'I know all that!' Arthur's face was red again, bright red. 'Look, the whole Princess Moldo plan depends on the hotel staff not suspecting a thing! If you burst in there and get caught then—'

'I'm not going to get caught, am I? Just guard the rope, Artie!'

'I don't need to! Just like you don't need to do this trick of yours!'

'I'll be back soon!'

'Harry! You're not listening to me again!'

'This is all for Herbie! That's what matters!'

'Of course it's about Herbie! Why else do you think me and Billie thought up our—'

'Remember the rope!'

'HARRY! STOP ACTING LIKE YOU DON'T WANT ANYTHING TO DO WITH ME! I'VE GOT ENOUGH OF THAT IN MY LIFE ALREADY!!'

Harry swung round. He saw his friend's face. He had never seen it look quite like it before. It was trembling all over. Artie's hand was trembling too, as it reached into his pocket and tore out a letter, the letter to the school, the one Harry had helped snatch just a few hours ago.

'NEXT THING, YOU'LL BE WANTING TO SEND ME 452 MILES AWAY TOO! YOU WON'T HAVE TO LISTEN TO ME THEN! IS THAT WHAT YOU WANT! IS IT? IS IT—'

'Whoah!'

Harry had lost his balance. He recovered it the only way he could, by swinging his foot right round and planting it on the rope out over the street. He was balanced again, but he had also started the walk, and he couldn't stop, he had to keep walking, walking out over the street. *Perhaps that's for the best.* The echoes of Artie's words were still shuddering around him, making his face burn—he had no idea how to reply. *Perhaps this way I don't have to— at least until I've thought of something to say.* His face still pulsing with heat, he angled his arms, steadied his legs, bit his lip. *Need to concentrate on the rope walk,* he told himself—because it was turning out to be harder, much harder, than the one in the park.

The breeze sweeping up from the street was surprisingly powerful, full of the distant sounds of the street below. Harry glanced down, and his heart throbbed as he made out the tiny shapes of people, horses, cabs. The breeze flapped through his clothes, buffeting him about, and each time he lifted a foot from the rope he had to adjust his position, leaning into the gusts so that they wouldn't blow him off. *Completely different from the park.* The wind was affecting the rope too, making it quiver, and it bounced slightly with every step. Harry's heart pounded and the palms of his hands, flung out on either side of him, were damp with sweat. He tried to think of nothing but his feet, edging along the rope step by step, and he carried on leaning slightly into the wind, letting it support him . . .

With no warning, it changed direction.

Harry's arms flailed. Desperately, he tried to right himself as he tilted off the rope, unable to regain his balance. The wind spiralled around him with its noises of the far-below street, and Harry watched his arms blur through the air, felt his heart hammer inside his chest, and then, just in time, shot out a trembling leg.

The shift of weight tilted him back, just a little. He re-angled his arms, and that helped too. The wind buffeted, his clothes flapped, the rope shuddered. He was balanced again, but only just. His legs were weak and trembling, and his face clenched as tight as a fist. *Concentrate, think of nothing but the rope.* And yet, even as Harry tried to do just that, he couldn't help noticing something, out of the corner of his eye.

A window, in a nearby building. It was level with him, ten storeys up. Someone was watching him from it. A face. White hair, white eyebrows, a pair of staring eyes. A pale-suited figure, two hands resting neatly on a windowsill. Whoever he was, he was watching Harry, and something made Harry start turning his head, to take in this figure properly, to see him more clearly.

The wind blew. Harry's arms sprang out on either side, but he was tilting off the rope again. His arms swirled, his heart pounded, his hands snatched at the empty air, as he fought to pull himself back. Out of the corner of his eye, he saw that the pale-suited figure had vanished from the window.

Leaving nothing but dark, empty glass.

# *Chapter 13*

Harry had only glimpsed his observer. But the observer himself had seen Harry plainly. Even now, as he stepped back up to the window, he continued to study the boy who, for some reason, was teetering on a rope stretched between two buildings, nearly ten storeys up in the air.

About eleven years old. A street boy, from the look of him. A shoeshiner, given certain dark blotches on his clothes and face which the observer had spotted, even at this distance.

The man stood at the window. His suit was elegantly tailored, its cloth cream. Neatly manicured fingers rested on the polished windowsill, and then rose to fetch a pen and a small leather notebook from their owner's pockets.

The boy had regained his balance. For the second time, he had nearly fallen, but his quick, nimble body had righted itself, and he was wobbling onward, making his way once more along the quivering rope. The man observed this, and made a quick sketch of the two buildings, the rope. Next to it, the pen dotted out several lines of complicated numerical code, along with another symbol, a very curious one indeed.

At first, it was just a circle. But the steel nib shaded inside it, until it was black with ink. Further up the pen's length, a finger twitched, flicking a tiny button. A hiss, as white mist leaked out of the pen's nib. The mist thickened, and drifted away.

Burned into the white circle, the white shape of a bird.

The boy had gone now. Only the rope remained. But the notes had been made. The man closed the leather book, revealing on its cover another white bird shape. He slid it back into his pocket with the pen.

One hand waved, dispersing any lingering traces of mist. Another lifted a telephone from the desk, and dialled a number.

The telephone's earpiece buzzed. A voice, in a language that wasn't English, muttered through the crackles.

'It is possible,' the man said. 'That we have discovered a Candidate.'

# Chapter 14

Harry toppled onto the roof. He clung to a chimney stack, shaking all over. His body was weak, his heart still pounded and when he lifted his hands from the chimney's brickwork he saw they had left behind the shape of his palms and fingers in sweat. But he had made it back to the hotel—where the secret behind Herbie's disappearance, he was sure of it, would lie. Steadied by the thought, he set off across the roof, weaving past more chimney stacks towards the hatch he had spotted from the other side.

Not even locked. Why would it be when there was no reason to think anyone could get onto a ten-storey-high roof? But the door to Room 760 would be locked, that was for sure. Harry pulled the hatch open, slid down the ladder inside, and arrived at the top of a stairwell. Clattering down it, he peered around in his usual way for any stray bits of metal, a nail, a pin, anything at all useful. Nothing in the stairwell but, as he reached the seventh floor and slid off down a corridor, he saw a row of framed paintings on the wall. He stopped, lifted one down, and plucked the nail out of the plaster. *A pick*. Hurrying on, he prepared to inspect the lock on Zell's door and bend the nail into the right shape, but then he reached the corner, peered round it, and saw that he didn't need a lock-pick after all.

The door to Room 760 was open. Next to it, a trolley of fresh linen stood, and two maids hurried into the room with fresh sheets. Harry tossed the nail away, and ducked under a table by the wall. Watching from under the tablecloth, he waited until the maids' backs were turned. He glided through the door and rolled under the bed . . .

. . . straight into a peacock feather, an umbrella and a pair of dark-lensed spectacles.

'Harry?! I don't believe it! What are you doing here?'

'I came down from the roof . . . OW!'

'Didn't Arthur find you? Didn't he tell you that we already had a plan?'

'Well, I . . . MMMPF!'

Billie was squashed under the bed. The springs above were close to her head, her silk dress and bonnet and umbrella were bulky, and her elbow had ended up in Harry's mouth, making it hard for him to speak. Another hand was right in front of his face, holding up a little slip of paper.

'Well, you better not interfere! This plan's working just dandy and I'm not having you wreck it!' She pushed the bit of paper closer. 'This is the seventh-floor linen-changing rota. Artie sweet-talked one of the maids who works the hotel and found it out, so we knew I could just slip in here, nice and easy. Course, I had to get up here quick, but that was no trouble, 'cos it took no time at all to check in— whenever they asked me questions I just answered in Spanish, which is what they speak down Peru way, and Artie gave me a few phrases to remember.' The Princess Moldo spectacles, made in Lima itself, tilted on her nose. 'So I get my key, I go up to my room, I walk straight on past it, and come up here instead. Pretty impressive, huh? So don't you try to interfere, you hear me?'

The elbow left Harry's mouth. But he wasn't sure what to say anyway. Point by point, Billie had removed any possible questions he might have had about Arthur's and her plan, which he could see really was a very good one.

'So how did you get in? You better not have been spotted!' Billie hissed.

'I . . . I came down from the roof,' he said. 'Threw a rope from the building next door. It was like the trick we did in the park, Billie—'

'You tightroped here?'

'Yes—ten storeys up! It'll work for getting out too, I think, as long as Artie follows his instructions—'

'Artie? Instructions? So you DID see him then!'

Harry stopped talking, as instantly as if the elbow had blocked his mouth again. But the Princess Moldo spectacles were even closer now, and he was glad their lenses were so dark, because he sensed the eyes behind would be staring at him in a very unfriendly way indeed.

'You saw him! So he WOULD have told you about our plan!'

'Yes but—'

'He told you . . . and you decided to come anyway. You ignored him!'

'I know . . .' Harry winced. 'Except—'

'Typical! Can't you see how he's going to feel about that? With that father of his—GRRMPF!'

The maids had hurried over to the bed, and so Billie had been forced to swallow her words. But her face was still right up front of Harry's, those dark lenses glinting. He tried to wriggle away, but the bed wasn't wide enough, and so the two of them were stuck there, unable to move, unable to speak, their noses less than an inch apart. For nearly a minute, they stayed like that, while the maids changed the sheets above, and delicately dusted nearby ornaments. But at last, the maids left, shutting the door behind them, and Harry scrambled out.

'I'm sorry . . . I—'

'What's got into you, Harry?' Billie scrambled out too. 'Running off all the time! Never listening to a word me and Artie say!'

'Herbie's been kidnapped! I can't just stand about—'

'Think me and Artie don't know that? We want to help Herbie too!'

'So let's rescue him!'

'That's what me and Artie are *doing*! That's what the Princess Moldo plan is all about, not that you've noticed! You know, Harry, when I met you and Artie, I thought you were the best friends I'd found since New Orleans—' The glasses trembled, their lenses flashed. 'Well, I was right about Artie—not so sure about you! All you care about is thinking up plans of your own like this tightroping business . . . Supposed to be impressed, am I?'

'It got me in here, didn't it?'

'But you don't *need* to be here! That's what I'm saying!'

'Of course I need to be here! Herbie's my friend.'

'HE'S OUR FRIEND TOO! WE'RE MEANT TO BE DOING THIS *TOGETHER*! WE'RE A TEAM, AREN'T WE? OH, CONFOUND IT!'

Harry ducked. Billie had hurled her silk umbrella straight at him, and he managed to dodge it, but only just. It smashed into the mantelpiece, splintering several of the ornaments the maids had so carefully dusted, and then flew off at an angle, thudding into a chair. Porcelain fragments fell from the mantelpiece, rocked on the floor, and went still.

'Billie?'

He swung round. Billie's arms were crossed, and those Princess Moldo glasses glared, but even worse was the fact that Billie, for the first time Harry could remember, seemed to have nothing more to say. She just stood there, wobbling a bit on her heightened shoes, the peacock feathers on her bonnet sticking out at angles. Then she flumped down into the nearest chair.

'Confound it, I say!'

Harry turned, and took in the hurled umbrella, the smashed porcelain too. He thought about Arthur too, back on the fire escape. *Enough of that in my life already* . . . Harry could hear those words now, as if they were echoing around him, and he winced again. 'Listen, Billie. I'm sorry—'

He broke off as he saw the briefcase.

'Oh no you don't, Harry! That's MINE!'

It stood by a desk on the other side of the room. Boris Zell's briefcase, the same one that Harry had seen on the bulky magician's knee, the one with the telltale wisp of smoke, and Harry was already gripping its handle. But Billie's hand was gripping it too, her Princess Moldo spectacles just an inch away from his nose again.

'I saw it first!' she spluttered.

'But—'

'Saw it the second I got in here!'

'Well, I saw it before that! Last night in the theatre! Remember?'

Harry couldn't let go. If anything would reveal the truth about what had happened to Herbie, it would be the contents of that briefcase. *Later on, I'll sort things out with Billie, and with Arthur too,* he decided. For now, it was the briefcase that mattered, and nothing else, and he tried to tug it free, and tugged harder, and harder still, and then wondered, too late, if that was a good idea.

'Watch out!'

He stumbled back. The briefcase had split open. A monkey skull, two candlesticks, and a heavy book tumbled onto the floor. But he wasn't worried about those. He watched as a corked jar of purple powder spun out of the briefcase too, slammed onto the floor, and cracked. A flash of light, the room thundered, and he was thrown straight into a wall.

Purple smoke, everywhere. Harry tasted the chemicals in his mouth again. He heard the sound of tinkling glass, and knew the window had blown out. At least he had ended up in a more comfortable position this time, sliding down onto the hotel room's rug rather than crashing into the sidewalk. Struggling up, he groped through the fumes, among which he made out Billie's face, along with a finger, pointing at him.

'Now look what you've gone and done!'

'You should have just let me open it carefully!'

'Why? I'm the one who's investigating this hotel room! Me—Princess Moldo, I mean!'

'Well, at least I was right about Zell.' Harry knelt over the shattered remains of the jar. 'He's behind the explosion in Herbie's dressing room, we know that for sure now.'

'Don't know too much else though.' Billie peered through the plumes of smoke. 'So Boris explodes something in the dressing room—but how'd he get in there? How'd he get out again, dragging Herbie too? No one saw nobody go in or out, remember?'

It was true. Harry sniffed the smoke. That was all it was—smoke. Billie was right, it told him nothing. Zell had kidnapped Herbie, he knew the magician's motive thanks to the telegram from Chicago. But how had he done it? That was the true mystery, and the smoke, still drifting around him, revealed nothing about it at all.

The plumes swirled. And the smoke *did* reveal something. Harry flinched, and the smoke he had sniffed flew out of his nostrils in two little clouds. Across the room, Billie was looking alarmed too.

There right in front of them, materializing out of the smoke, was Boris Zell.

# Chapter 15

'You! Boy from theatre!'

The huge magician's eyes glittered in the smoke. His accented voice boomed through the drifting plumes, making them thrash and swirl. Harry wondered if he really *did* have some sort of magical power. How else had he managed to appear so silently, as if summoned by the smoke? How had he managed to track him and his friends down at the library? But there really wasn't time to worry about any of that, because Zell, magical or not, was lunging through the smog, a burly hand outstretched, and it was time to run for it, as fast as he possibly could.

'Quick, Billie!'

No need to tell her. She was already running. Together they dodged through the smoke, ducked past the lunging arm, and tried to get through the doorway, tangling up in Billie's billowing silk dress and peacock-feathered bonnet. A knot of arms, legs, feathers, and genuine Peruvian spectacles, they thudded out onto the corridor floor.

'Out of my way, Harry!'

'I'm tangled up!'

'Bad enough you not letting no one else break into this place! Now you're not letting no one but you escape from it neither!'

'Just run!'

'Don't you tell me what to do!'

'Run!'

'I'm not taking orders from you no more!'

'RUN!'

Zell's arm swooped into the corridor. Billie scrambled along the hall, hopped up onto the banister of a nearby staircase, and slid down it. She crossed her arms, and those Princess Moldo spectacles remained fixed on Harry, glaring with rage as she gathered speed.

'Boy! You come here!'

*No time to think.* Zell was nearly upon him. The burly magician had lurched through the doorway, and Harry took off in the opposite direction from Billie, racing up the corridor. He could hear heavy gasps behind him, could feel the tips of those huge fingers touching the back of his jacket, but his legs sprang to life and he flew off down the corridor. He slammed into the stairwell and scrambled upwards. Spiralling up the steps, he heard a door slam below, and knew Boris was in the stairwell too, but he flew up the last flight of stairs to the ladder, burst through the hatch, and ran between the chimney stacks. He saw the roof's edge, and the tightrope stretching away, and his heart throbbed again at the thought of the walk that lay ahead—but he knew he had no choice. With a leap, he was up on the railing, a foot on the rope. He was ready, a single step would send him off on the journey across the street. He swung round for one last look at his terrifying foe.

Zell didn't seem quite so terrifying now. Across the roof, he was stumbling towards Harry, but slowly. Sweat poured off his face, winding into his moustache and making it droop. His burly arms drooped too, sapped of strength. Tottering, he gripped a chimney stack to keep himself upright.

'You were there that night!' He pointed feebly at Harry. 'The Wesley Jones Theatre . . . Maybe you saw something . . . Help me . . .'

'Why would I help you?' The words just flew out. 'You—you're behind it all! The smoke, the explosion, everything! You're the one who kidnapped Herbie.'

A mistake. Harry's lips clenched tight. But it was

too late, the words were already trembling through the air, and now Zell would know how much had already been discovered. *Better get on with the escape.* He turned back and took his first step along the rope, but then froze, as he heard Zell's next words.

'Kidnap Herbie? Why would I do that? Why would I do anything of the sort to a man . . . who is my oldest, dearest friend?'

Harry toppled. His feet fumbled and slipped.

And he fell straight off the rope.

# Chapter 16

Harry's hand caught the rope as he dropped. He jerked to a halt, and hung there, dangling. But his fingers' grip was already weakening. He stared down, and saw his feet swaying over the far-below street. He stared up, and saw his fingers, steadily losing their hold, the strength draining from them one by one . . .

He flew up through the air. A burly hand had circled his wrist, and he was being hoisted up onto the roof. He collapsed in a heap, and looked up to see Boris Zell releasing his wrist and sinking down onto the roof too, more exhausted-looking than ever. Harry tried to scrabble away.

'You're lying! Herbie's my friend! Not yours!'

'Believe what you like . . .' The heavily-accented voice was a feeble gasp. 'What do I care! You were my only clue, boy . . . But I was mistaken, I see that now . . .'

'Me? *Your* . . . clue?' Harry kept scrabbling, but his back was against the rail at the edge of the roof.

'The boy must have something to do with it, I think . . . Herbie disappears—and the next day I see a boy who was at the theatre when I visit a library . . . Strange, I think . . .'

'Not really! We had every reason to go to the library! We needed to find out information about you, didn't we? How come YOU were there—that's the strange thing!'

'I went to look up books about disappearing acts.' Zell shrugged. 'I cannot understand how Herbie was snatched away . . . I think maybe a book will tell me . . .'

*Not a bad answer,* thought Harry. The library would be full of such books—it might have been clever to have looked at a few himself.

His eyes kept darting about, searching for a way to escape. There were plenty of other things that needed explaining, and they would need answers every bit as good.

'Who cares about the library! What about the jar of purple smoke powder in your briefcase? The same purple smoke that went off that night in Herbie's dressing room!' Harry jabbed an accusing finger. 'Explain that, Boris Zell!'

Zell said nothing. He just crouched there, still recovering his breath. His moustache drooped even more forlornly. He wasn't to be trusted, Harry was sure of it.

'Purple smoke?' Boris sighed. 'The Magician's Fire, you mean. Very well, I shall explain it. It is a simple enough device. A powder that, when thrown to the ground, explodes into smoke—useful for magicians who wish to hide something from their audience. Other powders do this, but the Magician's Fire is a variety I mix myself, to achieve the attractive purple colour of the smoke.' He struggled up. 'It is not so dangerous, boy.'

*True enough*, thought Harry. He himself had just been caught in an explosion of it and it hadn't done any harm, just thrown him against a wall, smashed out a window, and clouded things up a bit. Clouded things up like Zell was doing now, perhaps? Remembering something, he pulled from his pocket the telegram from Oscar P. Munz, owner of the Chicago theatre.

'So, maybe the smoke isn't dangerous. But it still belongs to you. And it blew up in Herbie's room when he disappeared! How come something only you own ends up there that night?' He waved the telegram. 'And listen, I may not know how you kidnapped Herbie, but I know why. This tells me, plain as day.'

'Does it?' Boris stared at the telegram. Those cruel eyes, Harry noticed, bulged with a watery sheen.

'It's from the next theatre you're playing, in Chicago. It says you have agreed to perform Herbie's tricks there. Bicycling Over Spikes! The Flying Knives! Spider Up Sleeve! You kidnapped him to get the secret of those tricks! You've got him hidden somewhere, your prisoner until he tells you what you want to know.'

'We will talk about this one thing at a time, yes?' Zell stared intently at Harry. 'First, purple smoke. Why was it in Herbie's dressing room? The answer is simple, boy. I had given it to him just an hour before. A whole jar of Magician's Fire. A gift from me, Boris Zell, to my dear old friend.'

'Gave it to him?'

'Twenty years I have known Herbie Lemster.' Zell said. 'We meet backstage in a Prague theatre, when I was a penniless young magician. For a few weeks we travel together, him teaching me all he knew. *Dear Mr Herbie*, that is what I call him then, and that is what I call him ever after, whenever we meet again over the years that come, as we travel the roads of Europe. In theatres, in city squares, on platforms waiting for trains—we see each other and *Dear Mr Herbie*, I always say to him, and he always shakes my hand, he always smiles! To be travelling magician, it is not always easy, boy, and what greater comfort than a friend!' Boris hunched weakly. 'But our meetings were not to last.

'About three years ago, I notice it—I had not seen Mr Herbie for a while. Another month goes by, then another, then a year—I ask myself where is he? Is he ill? Does he perform magic no longer? I have no address for him, nor he for me, we are magicians of the road with no home to our name. I tell myself, I have lost my friend for ever!' Boris wiped the tears from his moustache. 'But my life goes on. My travels continue. In hope of finding Herbie, I journey further. To Moscow, St Petersburg, in the north. To Constantinople, in the south. More years go by. Like many magicians, I buy ticket for America, to carry on my travels there. I arrive in this city of New York, arriving just three days ago . . .'

*Interesting story*, thought Harry. Believable too— not least because of the speed at which it had flown from Boris's mouth, no hesitation or stuttering at all. Besides, a piece of information had caught his attention, a piece of information that, if true, might make this whole business very different indeed. Harry leaned closer, and listened with care.

'I check into this hotel,' Boris continued. 'I try to think how to set up business in this new country. I make telephone calls, I send telegram—yes, I will explain that, I promise.' He pointed at the telegram in Harry's hand. 'I make plans to tour Pittsburgh, to Buffalo, to Toronto, to Chicago. All day work, very hard. But then, at four o'clock yesterday afternoon . . .' For the first time, a smile appeared on Boris's face. 'I pick up a newspaper in the hotel lobby. Just by chance, you understand. I open it, and there is an advertisement for some Wesley Jones Theatre. It lists acts, a strong-man, dancers, so on. And there at the bottom, I see his name! Herbie Lemster, magician! Dear Mr Herbie, who I lose for so long, is here! I read his name! I throw newspaper in air! I go and find him! I look him up!'

'When exactly was that?' Harry walked over to Boris.

'Yesterday! Six o'clock. Just before evening show. I went to the stage door and asked for him but they told me that he was busy. But no matter, I go ahead with my plan anyway!'

'Your plan?'

'My plan to work with Herbie Lemster. No more meetings on road. We shall travel that road together! I write this to him in a note and leave it for him. I shake when I write, I am so excited! I say we meet after show. I leave a jar of Magician's Fire too—a gift for dear Mr Herbie. Then I go watch. I shake when I see Herbie again—I remember what good magician he is. But more, what a good friend he is. He and I, we will make success together, I know it! Show ends and I go to wait at stage door but then—BOOM! Magician's Fire explode! Herbie disappear!'

*It makes sense.* Every bit of Boris's story fitted neatly with what Harry knew. He spotted the snake on the burly man's cape, catching the sunlight. *A brooch, that's all—as for the Order of Gabrov, most magicians in Europe probably belong to a society of some kind.* Looking down, he noticed that the telegram was still in his hands, and he studied it thoughtfully.

'So the telegram from Chicago . . .'

'Ah yes.' Boris took the telegram from Harry. 'You think it strange that I say I can perform these tricks. You think, because they are Herbie's, that I must steal them, to make them my own? But why would I need to do such a thing? Herbie train me, remember? He teach me these tricks, one by one! He make me watch him, night after night, and bit by bit I spot things, work things out. It is the "Great Game Of Magic", Herbie says. These tricks, I have performed them all my life! Why wouldn't I write about them in telegram to Chicago?'

Harry scrunched the telegram into a ball and tossed it away. Everything he had thought about this business had turned out not to be the case, and he felt his face warm with a blush. But he stood up and walked about, letting the rooftop breeze cool him. No point in worrying about any of that. Apart from anything else, he had already spotted a whole new way of investigating the affair. His thoughts turned again to that little bit of information Boris had revealed just a few minutes ago.

'Mr Zell, you say you lost touch with Herbie about three years ago?'

'Why yes! Three years ago, yes!'

'Before that, for nearly twenty years, you saw him every few months?'

'Yes! In theatres. In city squares! In—'

'And, during all that time, you and Herbie—you were in Europe?'

'Yes! I already say this!'

'Not America, then?'

'No! Berlin, Paris, Prague . . . Only Europe! Why you ask this? And why you walk like that?'

Harry was pacing circles around Boris. He regarded him from every angle, and he considered what the magician had said from every angle too. It was the clue he needed, the telltale bulge, the tiny twitch that would give the whole trick away. He thought it through. According to Boris, Herbie Lemster had been working as a magician in Europe until just three years ago. Harry saw no reason to disbelieve him, it fitted in with

everything else he said. But it didn't fit with something
someone else had said, and that someone was . . .

*Wesley Jones.*

Wesley Jones, owner of the Wesley Jones Theatre.
The plump gentleman had said that Herbie had been
working happily for his theatre here in New York for
the last *ten* years. *'Why, I count him as one of my dearest
friends!'* Harry thought back to that conversation in the
theatre owner's office. He remembered it quite clearly,
he was sure of that.

'Boy? You make me dizzy!'

Harry was pacing even faster. Boris had become a
blur but he wasn't thinking about him any more. He
was thinking about each and every word he had heard
earlier that day as he crouched polishing those twenty
pairs of shoes. How distressed the theatre owner had
seemed. How bewildered by what had taken place.
How forcefully he had said, several times, that he and
his stage manager cared deeply for the performers
at their theatre, how they were even installing a new
plumbing system for their comfort—and, most importantly, how one performer, Herbie Lemster, had been
so happy at the theatre that he had worked there for
*ten* years—which now turned out to be untrue. Wesley
had lied. But why? What did it mean? Harry had no
idea, but he could feel a strange coldness spreading

through him, and he pulled his jacket close, but it kept spreading, the more he thought about Herbie, and that conversation with Wesley Jones . . .

'It's him! Look!'

'The boy! The one who threw himself out of the window!'

'Get him!'

The hotel porters. Far across the roof, they were clambering out of the hatch, two of them. Wisps of purple smoke rose from their clothes—clearly, they had been alerted by the explosion in Room 760. Boris could explain everything, but how long would that take? *Lost enough time already.*

'Boy! What you doing? You crazy?' shouted Zell.

Harry felt bad about Boris. He had only just started getting to know him and, far from being menacing, he seemed pretty friendly. But there really was no time—the porters were already stumbling between the chimney stacks and he needed to be quick. With a leap, he was at the railing again, balanced on the rope. His boots dangled around his neck, his arms wavered at his sides, and he was high over the street, one foot following the other, even faster than before . . .

'Come back, boy!' Zell's cry echoed after him. 'I already had to rescue you! Stop! Stop—'

'I'll be careful! It's for Herbie's sake, Mr Zell!'

Harry's feet flashed along the rope. The wind blew, the rope shuddered, the horses and people and cabs looked just as tiny down on the street below. But for some reason his legs didn't feel so weak this time, his heart wasn't pounding so fast, and his feet were picking up speed. He wondered if it was because he had done the tightrope walk one time before, had even survived a fall from it, thanks to Boris Zell. Perhaps that was why he felt more confident now, surer in his step. But he knew there was another reason too, a reason that burned deep inside him, powering him on . . .

*Get to the theatre.*

A gust of wind buffeted him, but he was ready. When it swung round behind him, he even used it, letting it push him along. His fists clenched, his feet kept flashing along, and he was already halfway. The rope bounced with every step, but Harry decided to use that too, letting the energy in the rope spring him along, powering him faster. Why, he wasn't just tight-rope-walking, he was tightrope-*running*—and a good thing too. *Get to the theatre.* Only a few steps left, and he took them even faster, leaping, springing along the rope, and landing with a neat chime on the iron fire escape . . .

. . . where he was knocked straight off his feet by Arthur, racing down the stairs.

# Chapter 17

'Harry! What were you doing on the roof—OW!'
Arthur tumbled down the fire escape. 'I was watching
you.'

'You were?' Tangled up with his friend, Harry tumbled too.

'Yes! I saw you! With Boris Zell! OUCH!'

'I was talking to him—'

'I know you were talking! But what about? I couldn't
hear—LOOK OUT!'

They were gathering speed. Harry watched Arthur's
face blur past, and snatched at the railings, but he was
travelling too fast. He tumbled onwards, and made out
a familiar voice, and some footsteps, clanging up the
steps.

'So I got out easy, Harry! No fancy tightrope-walking needed by me! The Princess Moldo trick, that's all!
I just walked out through the lobby, cool as a cucum-

ber, nobody asking me a single question! Not that you care about that—OOOF!'

They slammed right into her. Billie must have seen them coming, but their speed had clearly taken her by surprise, and she was part of their tangle now, tumbling downwards. The silk dress ripped, the bonnet crumpled, the peacock feathers flew through the air, and a flail of Harry's arm tore the Princess Moldo glasses right off Billie's face. They had snagged on his jacket's sleeve and he tried to pull them off, hoping to give them back to her, but they were too firmly lodged, one of the wire arms twisted through the lining.

'Don't look so surprised, Harry. You've wrecked the plan—why not wreck the costume as well?'

'I didn't mean to wreck . . . I was just trying to . . . OW!'

They had toppled down onto one of the fire escape landings, Harry slamming his head hard against its rails. He sprawled there, and wondered if he was still falling, because his head was spinning so fast. He stumbled up, and immediately fell down again. His head throbbed, his vision blurred, but he just about managed to make out his friends, still tangled up with him.

'You should have left it to me and Artie!' Billie sat up first, grabbing her bonnet from Arthur's foot and jamming it on her head again. 'If you hadn't blundered in and set off that explosion of smoke, I'd probably still be up there! Spying on Boris from under the bed! I'd have found out all kinds of things! Instead we've all of us found out nothing! Diddley-squat!'

'You're wrong about that, Billie—I actually think Harry might have found out quite a bit!' Arthur tugged at a peacock feather in his hair. 'He's been up on the hotel roof for nearly ten minutes talking with Zell. I saw them.'

'Really?' Billie spluttered.

'Not that he's told me much about it, mind.' Arthur frowned. 'Have you, Harry?'

'I'm sorry . . .' Harry gasped, still struggling to get up. 'I . . .'

'So tell us now, Harry!' Billie grabbed Harry's sleeve. 'It's the least you owe us after what you've done—especially to Artie!'

'It's true.' Arthur hesitated, and folded his arms. 'I'm sorry I got angry before, Harry—but I meant what I said. My whole life, I've been treated like I'm nothing important. Meeting you and Billie—well, it's the first time I've felt I'm actually somebody . . .'

'True of all of us!' Billie gripped Harry's sleeve tighter. 'What would I be without the two of you to help? A scruffy New Orleans street girl, doing crummy jobs and struggling to get by, that's all! As for you, Harry, where would you be if me and Artie hadn't noticed your tricks? So tell us! TELL US WHAT HAPPENED!'

'I'll try . . . It's not easy . . . I don't understand most of it myself yet . . .' At last, Harry managed to stumble up. He tried to make out his friends more clearly, but his vision was too blurred. And he tried to take in everything they had said, but his head was still spinning. 'I'm sorry Artie, of course I think you're important . . . I . . .' *Get to the theatre.* His head spun even faster, as he stumbled off down the fire escape towards the street below. 'I'll try to explain . . . Boris Zell . . . He's different from what I thought . . .'

'Different how?' Billie clanged after him, and Arthur wasn't far behind.

'Well, he's Herbie's friend . . .' Waves of dizziness swept over him.

'Friend? Why did he kidnap him then?'

'He didn't . . .' *Get to the theatre.*

'Who did then?'

'I don't know . . . Not yet . . .'

'What exactly did Boris say? You've got to tell us, Harry!'

Harry's head spun faster. His stomach throbbed, deep inside, and he thought he was going to throw up. The iron struts of the fire escape were a blurred jumble, the words in his head were a jumble too. He had to get away from his friends' questions, however much he wanted to answer them, because each one was only making him dizzier. Even if he managed to stutter something out, that would only lead them to ask more questions, needing more answers, taking longer and longer—and how would that help Herbie? *Get to the theatre,* he thought, *that's the only thing that matters,* and he stumbled down onto the fire escape's next landing.

'I'll tell you as soon as I can . . . It's too complicated . . . There isn't time . . . Herbie, he's in trouble . . . I've got to go . . . I . . .'

He saw, rattling along the street towards him three storeys below, the Number 47 streetcar.

'Harry!'

'Come back!'

He was throwing himself off the fire escape. With a life of its own, his fist was gripping the iron rail. His arm straightened, his body swung and he was tumbling down towards the rattling streetcar's roof twenty feet below. He thudded onto the roof, just inches away from the deadly overhead cables, and sprawled there as the streetcar rattled away, sparks showering around him. Still dizzy, he sat up, and looked back.

'I'm sorry . . .'

The words were snatched by the wind. His friends back on the fire escape clearly hadn't heard them at all. Billie pounded about on the landing; Arthur tore the peacock feather out of his hair and threw it to the ground. All around them lay the wreckage of their carefully-put-together costume, the squashed bonnet, the torn dress. Remembering the Princess Moldo spectacles, genuinely made in Lima itself, Harry fumbled with his jacket and managed to untangle them at last. Both lenses were smashed, and the wire-frames were bent out of shape. He tried to bend them back, but fragments of glass just fell out of the frames. *How can it have ended up like this?* he thought, as he looked back up at the two shapes on the fire escape, his friends. But they were too far away to make out properly now. He slid the broken glasses back in his pocket. He would give them back to them later. *Perhaps that'll make things better*, he told himself.

Although, as he rattled off across Manhattan to the Wesley Jones Theatre, he thought it probably wouldn't.

# Chapter 18

The streetcar clattered past the Wesley Jones Theatre, and Harry jumped off. He touched his head and felt a swelling bruise, but the dizziness was nearly gone, and it carried on fading as he slid into the laughing, chattering crowd that was pouring out from the theatre's afternoon show. No shoeshine plan necessary to get backstage this time—just a simple break-in was needed. He weaved through the crowd until he was in the foyer and glanced about, searching for a way. Seeing a door, he ducked across, checked that no one was looking, and pushed the handle up. Not even locked. He slid through, and closed the door behind him.

He was in a dimly lit corridor. He climbed a rickety staircase. More corridors, more staircases flashed by, and pipes, hundreds of them, throbbed and wobbled around him. Harry stared at them because almost everything Wesley had said seemed suspicious now, and the stuff about the plumbing improvements was no exception. Finding another staircase, he recognized it as the one he had climbed with Wesley Jones that morning and swiftly scrambled to the door at the top, placed an ear against it and, checking no one was inside, crept in.

*'He has worked happily at this theatre for no less than ten years . . .'*

Harry stood in the middle of Wesley Jones's office. He saw the plush rug, the cupboard containing the twenty pairs of shoes. The theatre owner's words echoed back to him—words which Harry now knew to be not entirely true. Why had Wesley lied? Why had he exaggerated the length of time Herbie had worked here? Could it be that he wished to make the old magician's happiness with his job at the theatre as convincing as possible? If so, why? The coldness Harry had felt on the roof crept into him again, and he started pacing the room, partly to keep warm, partly to help himself think. Five times, he circled the office, and then he dropped into Wesley Jones's leather chair, positioning himself just as the theatre owner had earlier that day, sliding into the curved hollow left by that plump figure—unpleasant but worth it, if it helped him see things from Wesley's point of view.

*'He considers this place his home sweet home . . .'*

The mantelpiece. There in front of Harry, as he sat in Wesley's chair, was that carved marble bulk, with its framed photographs of the performers running along the top. All through his weeping, Wesley had been staring right at those photographs, but why? Harry was out of the chair, inspecting the mantelpiece, lifting each photograph frame. His brain still couldn't piece together this business, but for the moment his fingers were doing the thinking. They scurried about, checking the frames, exploring the edge of the mantelpiece too. From its frame, Herbie's face peered out, as mysterious and wrinkled as ever . . .

Harry's fingers brushed against something.

On the underside of the mantelpiece, just beneath Herbie's photograph, a bump, a metal tip. Harry's fingers explored, and managed to grip its edge. He pulled, and an inch-long stub of metal slid out, a hinge at its base. *Some sort of switch.* He flicked it, and toppled back as the whole mantelpiece swung out from the wall, its heavy marble bulk moving smoothly and silently, supported on huge iron hinges that glistened with oil. Harry sprawled on the plush rug, staring at the dark doorway that had been revealed, before scrambling up and springing into the gloom.

A spiral staircase. Harry clattered down it, his hand clutching the rail. Light from Wesley's office spilled down from above, revealing crumbling walls, rotten timbers and yet more throbbing pipes. Harry heard the roar of the water inside them, and wondered again about the plumbing work Wesley had mentioned, and whether it was really just to improve the running water in the dressing rooms.

He plunged deeper into the gloom. The only light came from an iron lamp, dangling from a chain, with a candle flickering inside. The stairs led down to a windowless room, and it seemed to be full of water: black, rippling, the candlelight glimmering on its surface. Harry bent down and dipped his hand in the water. Icily cold. Harry flinched, and flinched again as, right in the middle of the water-filled gloom, he made out—a cage.

It was large, rectangular and made of iron. Across the front of it, Harry noticed some iron letters too. Candlelight flickered weakly off them but he couldn't quite make them out.

He stared at a figure inside the cage, knee-deep in water. Knotted ropes criss-crossed his body and a gag distorted his face but Harry recognized him immediately.

It was Herbie.

# Chapter 19

*Bicycling Over Spikes. The Flying Knives, Spider Up Sleeve.*
Harry remembered all his old friend's tricks and how
they had fascinated him. But none of them had ever
made him feel as astonished, and horrified too, as he
felt now, seeing Herbie in the cage. Standing at the
bottom of the stairs, the black water lapping at his
boots, it took him some time to realize that the old
man was jiggling in his chair, staring at him with bulg-
ing eyes, and trying to say something.

'Mmmmmmph!'

Harry splashed into the water. It reached halfway
up his legs, but he waded to the cage and gripped its
bars. Herbie's mouth was struggling to shape words
around the cloth gag, and Harry wondered if he could
somehow read those struggling lips, and tried to do
that, only to realize that the frail magician was jerking
his head back towards the dangling iron lamp. Harry

splashed over and found, just next to the candle, a key. Twisting it in the lock, he slid the door across and waded into the cage. He tried to undo the old man's gag, but the knot securing it was tight; he tugged at it, prised at it, and finally pulled it loose, only to collapse back into the water with a splash, knocked off balance by the force of the old man's cry.

'Harry! What are you doing here? You are in danger! Don't you realize?'

Harry sprawled in the water. Soaked, he struggled back up. Herbie's cry still echoed, but the power of it seemed to have exhausted the old man, and he was slumped in his chair. Harry's fingers probed the ropes that held his friend, their knots even tighter than the gag's. He worked them, and tried to answer Herbie's questions.

'I'm here to rescue you, Herbie. I watched the window of your dressing room—saw what happened before you disappeared. I thought Boris Zell was behind it but . . .'

'Boris?' The old man's face lifted, his eyes shimmering. All that was left of his voice was a feeble gasp. 'Why would Boris do such a thing? He is my oldest friend—'

'I know that now.' Harry kept working at the knots. 'You trained him. You met each other all over Europe! You saw each other at theatres, in city squares—'

'If only I had stayed in Europe,' wailed Herbie. 'If only I had never come to New York . . . If only I had never set eyes on the Cruel Theatre Of Wesley Jones!'

Tears travelled down the complicated pathways of the old man's wrinkled face. His lips trembled, and went still; a sorry sight. Harry hoped that Herbie would gather enough strength to continue with his tale soon. Clever though it had been to discover the mantelpiece trick, he still had no idea of what was going on, and so far his elderly friend's gasps had just confused things further.

'The Cruel Theatre Of Wesley Jones? What do you mean?'

'I signed Wesley's contract in desperate times . . .' The gasps could only just be heard. 'I had fallen ill on the journey across the Atlantic, and for nearly a month after arriving in this hard city I could not work—I was penniless! So when I met Wesley, I signed. I agreed to perform at his grubby theatre for a grubby wage, show after show, night after night. But no one gets out of Wesley's contracts, I know that now . . .'

'How come?'

'Because Wesley Jones never lets go of a talented performer! Once his grip has you, it never relents! All of us at this theatre, we are forced to perform endlessly for a pittance, but no one dares leave. Some, he has tricked into debt, and if they dare defy him he will have not only them but anyone they might hold dear thrown out on the street, penniless. Others, he controls thanks to harbouring little secrets from their past, petty crimes or shameful doings, proof of which he keeps filed away in a hidden safe—again, if they defy him, he will destroy them utterly! What power he has!' The old man clutched his throat, every word causing him pain. 'And then there are those, such as myself, whom he controls by sheer menace alone. Desperate, we wish to leave this dreadful place. And yet we dare not, for fear of what would happen if we tried. A terrible threat hangs over us . . .'

'What?' Harry was trying to take it all in.

'What? Who, you mean. Why, Arnold, of course! Stage manager . . . and notorious failed trapeze artist!'

Harry's fingers tore at the knots. Each one was more intricate than the last, but he was prying them loose, and the terrible business of Herbie's disappearance was unravelling too. Harry remembered his conversations with the theatre's performers, and how mournful they had been about Herbie—well, perhaps they were sad for other reasons too? As for Arnold, the gangly stage manager with his weakened leg seemed an unlikely threat, but Harry also remembered that moment when Arnold had shown him out of the theatre and had gripped his shoulder with surprising strength.

'Failed trapeze artist? But Wesley Jones said he was a successful one, who injured himself years ago . . .'

'He injured himself trying to outdo all other performers.' Herbie glanced fearfully around the gloom. 'Fell from the trapeze and damaged his left leg beyond repair—but that doesn't mean the rest of him isn't strong and fit. Every one of Arnold's limbs, apart from that left leg, harbours a trapeze artist's strength—a strength gone wild from frustration at his thwarted performer's ambition.' The voice kept going, a tangle of whimpers and sobs. 'Unable to thrill audiences any longer, he nurses a profound hatred of anyone who can. Any of us who dares step out of line, Wesley sends Arnold to their dressing room, and they quickly regret it. As for any of us who dares to go near another theatre to discuss possible work—why, Arnold finds out and the regrets are more pitiful still! The sorry offender is dragged down to this terrible place . . . With its terrible words . . .'

'Words? What do you mean?'

'Why the motto Wesley snarls at us, his enslaved performers, every day.'

A terrified finger pointed up. Harry looked up too, at the iron letters on the cage. They gleamed in the candlelight, and now he made them out quite clearly. *'What's yours is mine and always shall be.'* Harry stared, and remembered hearing those very words, trembling through Herbie's dressing room window as the mysterious intruder grappled with the spindly old man. His fingers tore at the intricate knots with even greater speed.

'Wesley's control is total! Like a gangster, his menaces hold us in line! I tried to shield you from it, Harry! Why else do you think I never let you backstage? Or met you after a show at the stage door? Were you to have accidentally discovered Wesley's secret . . . Why, who knows to what lengths Wesley would go to protect himself? I would never have even befriended you, were it not for the memories you, a budding young trickster, brought back to me of happier times . . .' Herbie's words gasped on. 'For years I suffered this grim existence. I wasted my talents on Wesley's brutal stage. A couple of times, I tried to find other work in New York but Arnold found me, and my punishment was swift—four days down here the first time, a week the second. Once, I even tried to fly the city, but both times Arnold snared me before I even reached the train station, and I was down here for another week. After that, I resigned myself to working at Wesley Jones's cruel theatre for evermore.' His head sank, grey hair trailing. 'That was until late yesterday afternoon when . . .'

'Your old friend, Boris Zell, left you a letter.' Just one knot left.

'A miracle! Normally, Arnold checks all letters, but Boris, purely by chance, had tucked the letter inside a parcel containing a jar of his Magician's Fire, a gift to me. Arnold tore open a bit of the wrapping, assumed it was merely equipment, and let me have it. And indeed, a jar of Magician's Fire was a most welcome gift, but it was the letter, and the offer in it, which caused me most delight.' Feebly, Herbie looked up. 'The thought of returning to the freedom of a life on the road again with my dear old friend Boris by my side . . . why, it awakened hopes and desires that I simply could not contain. Despite Wesley, despite that tyrannical trapeze artist, I foolishly decided to risk it all one final time . . .'

'You decided to escape—after the performance last night!' Two fingernails gripped the last loop of knot. 'Was that why you looked so strange when we saw you before the show? You must have just received Boris's note! You were trembling and pale and . . .'

'Of course I was! I was terrified! But I was also determined, fool that I am! I packed my bags. I didn't say a word to a soul. I cleared my room of all props and equipment I might need to take with me. My feeble hope was to sneak out through the front of the theatre, while Arnold was distracted down at the stage door. He always liked to show off there with Wesley after a performance—'

'But Wesley sent him up to find you! So . . .' Just a couple of strands remained, but they were stubbornly intertwined. 'But I was watching your dressing room. I saw what happened! And the man I saw with you was big, Herbie. Not thin like Arnold.'

'The slant of the light, boy.' Herbie shook his head. 'Any decent magician would tell you a shadow cast upon a window is far larger than its source. No, it was Arnold all right. He burst in just as I was about to leave—the trapeze artist's grip had me once again!' More tears trickled along the wrinkles. 'I was forced to the ground and I heard him scream his master's words . . .'

*'What's yours is mine and always shall be! You remember that, Herbie Lemster!'* Harry repeated the words, as his fingernails worked the final strands.

'He forced me to the floor! Desperate, I thought of all I would miss, of a life with my dear friend Boris— the sheer misery gave me the strength to fight back the only way I could. With—'

'Boris's jar of Magician's Fire! You threw it at Arnold, it exploded and—'

'Smoke everywhere! The window shattered! Arnold was thrown to the ground and knocked his head and, for a few seconds, I thought I might be free! What madness!' The tears overflowed the wrinkles, seeping across Herbie's face. 'Through the purple mist, that trapeze artist's grip had me once again! Out of my dressing room I was bundled—'

'And the other performers saw you, of course they did!' The final strand broke lose, and the ropes slithered away. 'But they were too terrified to say anything. They knew the same thing would happen to them!'

'Along the corridor, into Wesley's office . . .' The last remnants of strength faded from Herbie's voice. 'Down, down, down here . . .'

It all made sense. Harry hurled the ropes away. No magical disappearance—just the brutal bundling of a feeble old man down a corridor. Bruno the Strongman and all the others had sworn they hadn't seen a thing, but only because they were as terrified as Herbie. As for everyone who had searched the theatre—who would have thought to have looked beneath the mantelpiece in Wesley Jones's office, or had fingers nimble enough to have detected that hidden switch? Herbie, weak from being tied so long, slithered off the chair into the water. Harry grabbed the old man's arm, pulled him up, and together they stumbled out of the cage.

'Don't worry, Herbie. I'll rescue you!'

'But how? How will you do that . . .'

'I'll get you out of here for a start!'

'All on your own? But . . . What about young Billie? And Arthur? They are waiting to help, perhaps?'

'Not really . . .' Harry realized that, for some time now, he hadn't had the slightest thought of his friends.

'But why? You are always together, the three of you!' The old man's voice sounded strangely hysterical. 'You don't mean to say you came here alone?'

'Well, yes . . .'

'At least tell me they know where you are. You told them, didn't you?'

'I don't think so . . .'

'Stop right there, shoeshine boy!' said a familiar voice.

Harry looked up, even as Herbie slithered out of his grasp and dropped back into the water. There, standing at the bottom of the stairway, were Wesley Jones and Arnold.

# *Chapter 20*

Everything Herbie had said about Arnold's trapeze artist's strength was true. With a single lop-sided stride the stage manager was on him, his spindly limbs locking him in a hold. Harry fought back, but every move was blocked by a steely hand, and he realized that he was upside down, the water, the iron steps flying underneath him as he was effortlessly carried up the stairs. A flash of light, and he was back in Wesley's office. The slam of a cupboard door, and it was dark again.

'Think you'd help out ol' Herbie, did ya? And all the other no-good performing folk who work here, I'll be bound! Well, you ain't doing no such thing. Me and Mr Jones, we're who decides what goes on round here. Now don't you say a word, boy!'

A bony hand over Harry's mouth made sure of that. Arnold had slammed himself in the cupboard too, but his face could just be made out in the gloom, those normally wide-open eyes tightened into narrow slits, staring furiously. Harry stared back. His heart was pounding faster than he had ever known. It felt like a knife, jabbing into him with every beat.

*Billie and Arthur.* He saw them, their blurred faces as they tumbled together down the fire escape. Desperately, his mind flew back over that strange, muddled conversation again, thinking of every word that had been spoken, of every tiny gesture that had been made. Had he said anything about where he was going? *No, nothing at all.* As far as Billie and Arthur were concerned, he was just off on another bit of the investigation. They would have no idea . . .

*That he needed their help very badly indeed.*

'I dare say you know I ain't been so pleased with you, Herbie.' Footsteps, and Wesley's voice was heard through the cupboard door. 'A day in the Punishment Chamber tends to make people aware of how I see 'em.'

'Yes, Mr Jones . . .' Herbie's broken voice managed a few words.

'But I never stay in a funk for too long.' A well-oiled clunk, as the mantelpiece swivelled shut. 'That boy wasted his time in so many ways. I was always intending to release you around now. Why, I need my star act to take the stage again . . . DON'T I?'

The thud of a plump fist down on a desk. From Herbie, a wheeze.

'Yes Mr Jones! Of course!'

'Now, that boy. Friend of yours, is he?'

'Yes . . .'

'He's going to have a lucky escape. As we speak, that very boy is running as fast as he can down the street outside, our stage manager right after him. Arnold'll give him a fair licking, but he'll let him go, course he will. Friend or not, I don't think that boy's gonna be troubling us again, do you Herbie?'

'No Mr Jones . . . Thank you . . .'

Herbie's voice was a gasp of fear, but also of relief. But Harry knew something far worse than a licking was in store for him, and he fought against Arnold's grip with even greater force, his heart jabbing so hard that his eyes watered with pain. His muscles strained, his limbs tried to wriggle their way out of Arnold's grip, and his mind was wriggling even faster, going through those last moments on the fire escape. *They won't even have been surprised,* he thought. *It's not as if they're not used to me running off, is it?* In the cupboard's darkness, Harry felt his face burn again, as he thought of everything that had happened. *The hurled umbrella. The smashed pieces of porcelain.* Worst of all, Arthur's outburst on the fire escape. *'Enough of that in my life already . . .'*

Harry shook his head from side to side, but the memory of those words stayed in there, painfully lodged.

The cupboard door flew open. Herbie was gone, and Harry was out of the cupboard, Arnold's trapeze artist limbs still wrapped around him. The mantelpiece slid open on its hinges, Harry fought, but Arnold bundled him back into the dark. The candle stub flickered, the black water rippled, the cage door slid shut. Harry flung himself against the iron bars. He prised at the lock. His eyes flicked about, his fingers twitched, as a tiny part of him wondered if he could play that little game, the one where he searched out some stray bit of metal, one that he could bend into the correct shape to pick a lock. But he wasn't going to find any bit of stray metal, was he? *Not trapped here, in a water-filled cage.* Staring at the spiral staircase, he saw Wesley Jones making his way down, rotating his pink top hat between his thumbs.

'The Punishment Chamber is my usual name for this place.' Wesley was at the foot of the stairs. His face was as plump as ever, but the lips were slightly apart and the teeth behind were surprisingly sharp. 'You interfered with my theatre, boy. Do you have any idea how hard it is, running a theatrical establishment in this city? Many would say I manage things the only sensible way.'

'You told me Herbie was happy!' Harry heard a voice ring out, unusually high-pitched, and could hardly believe it was his own. 'You said he was a friend of yours for ten years! You said he and all the other performers love working here but—'

'Sure, I lied.' The lips revealed a few more teeth. 'You haven't been in New York very long, have you?'

A lever clanked. Arnold was next to the foot of the stairs, knee-deep in water, and he was tugging a lever, while making various adjustments to it with one of the spanners from his leather bag. Another clank, and water flooded out of the various pipes that sprawled around the room's clammy walls. Churning, the black water began circling the cage. And it wasn't just circling, Harry noticed.

It was rising.

'You didn't really believe that you, a mere boy, could bring down the Wesley Jones Theatre?' The pink hat twirled once more. 'A theatre which I, an experienced vaudevillian, have engineered so carefully to operate with precision. Patiently, expertly, I have broken my performers' spirits, while preserving all that makes them so valuable, namely, their skills. Less a theatre, more an ingeniously assembled machine—and I am powerfully proud of it. The idea that you could bring such careful work crashing down is absurd.'

'I'll tell everyone what you're doing!' Harry heard that high-pitched voice again.

'Well, yes, that *might* bring it all crashing down.' Wesley put his head on one side, as if finding the idea genuinely intriguing. 'But my point still stands because there is no chance whatsoever of you doing that, shoe-shine boy.' He nodded at Arnold. 'The second lever, Arnold?'

'Right away, Mr Jones!' Arnold held up another spanner, lolloped up the stairs, and went to work.

'As I mentioned before, the Punishment Chamber is my usual name for this contraption.' Wesley turned back. 'Every now and then, however, a different title is needed. Wesley's Whirlpool, that's what I call it then.'

Halfway up the stairs, Arnold grabbed another lever. He twirled the spanner, loosened a bolt, and crunched the lever down. The whole staircase shuddered and, in the middle of the swirling, rising water, the cage shuddered too.

'I never liked that boy, Mr Jones!' Arnold dropped the spanner back into his bag, sneering. 'Remember how he talked to me about being such a great fan of the theatre? Dreams of being a performer himself, I'll be bound.'

'Ah, but it is one thing to dream of a life upon the stage, another thing to achieve such a life!' Wesley nodded. 'Or, in the case of this boy, to hang on to any life at all.'

The cage was still shuddering. The bars were throbbing, and when Harry gripped them, they turned his fists to white blurs. Something directly under his feet thudded, and the cage began to grind downwards.

'Now, I daresay, theatrical fellow that you are, you are expecting this machine to be a spectacular one. A fanciful contraption against which you can pit your wits—deadly piranhas or electric eels, perhaps? I'm sorry to disappoint you. This machine is merely a plumbing device.' Wesley headed back up the stairs. 'All theatres, no matter how carefully run, require occasional cleaning. Once in a while, they get clogged, if you like, by an unwanted item, a foreign body—something that needs to be flushed out. You, my boy, are such an item, and Wesley's Whirlpool is the plumbing tool that will flush you away, while Arnold and I attend to a far more important affair, the preparation of this evening's show. The cage you are in is moving downwards and the water, you will have noticed, is swirling upwards in a whirlpool-like style. The result, regarding you, I am sure you understand. Afterwards, sluices will open and this room and all its contents, including those that remain in the cage, will sweep straight out to the Hudson river, and flow away from this great city of ours, towards the sea . . .'

'You can't do this!'

'Is that what you think? You really *haven't* been in New York for long.' Wesley returned his hat to his head. 'Nor, by the process I have just described, will you be for very much longer.'

He trod up the stairs and, together with Arnold, disappeared into the gloom.

# Chapter 21

Harry flung himself at the bars. He pulled at them, kicked them, but the cage carried on grinding steadily down. *Think of something.* He watched the cage's lock sink below the surface, ducked down, and peered at it in the watery darkness. Was there a chance, the ghost of a chance, that he might be able to find some bit of metal after all? Something to bend into a pick? *Impossible.* The only metal was the cage itself, welded and bolted together. Beneath its base, Harry made out a steadily turning iron cog, its teeth levering the contraption downwards. Reaching through the bars, he tried to stop it with his fingers, but the teeth tore through his skin, and a trembling bubble flew out of his mouth, a shout of pain. He burst back to the surface, his hand bleeding. His body cold and numb, he could no longer feel his heart jabbing. He just shuddered, as it slammed against the inside of his chest.

*Billie and Arthur.* He saw their faces again, hovering in the blackness. *What would they be doing now if they had any idea what was happening,* he thought, and he knew the answer immediately. Despite everything, they would be racing across Manhattan, and they would be making up a plan, and it would be a good one too. He could see them now, their determined expressions, and he could hear their voices . . . He heard other sounds as well, the clatter of plates and spoons and, even more strangely, he felt a patch of warmth on each of his hands, even as they gripped the icy bars. He saw his friends again. They were at a table now, the one in that grimy diner, crumbs of chocolate sponge scattering on the cloth. Billie and Arthur were holding each other's hands, and they were holding the hands of their other friend, the one across the table . . .

*The one who they'll never see again.*

The water was up to his chest. He ducked back under it and reached for the cog again, but the teeth tore through his skin even faster this time. Another bubble of pain, and he shot back up out of the water, so fast that his head hit the bars at the top of the cage. He gripped them, and the vibrations shuddered through his bones. One last time, he saw Billie and Arthur. They were back sitting at the bottom of that fire escape again, the Princess Moldo costume in ruins, the dress ripped, the bonnet squashed. Why, thanks to him, Billie had even lost the very best bit of it, the Princess Moldo spectacles, genuinely made in Peru, and knocked off by his arm during the fall down the fire escape—

*The Princess Moldo spectacles.*

Harry's hand flew under the water. He dug inside his jacket, the pocket to the left. The spectacles were still there, where he had slid them, as he rattled away on the streetcar. He hadn't thought about them much then, apart from deciding he would give them back to his friends when he could. But he was thinking about them now. He had never thought about anything so intently in his life.

He lifted them up. The dark lenses were smashed; the frames were bent. But the thin arms were still intact.

*Arms with curved, bendable metal ends.*

Harry sucked in another gulp of air and dived under the water. He tore off one of the spectacle arms and sank towards the iron cog. With his still-bleeding hand, he angled the curved length of metal between the teeth and watched it catch hold. The cage shuddered to halt, although the spectacle arm wouldn't hold long, and the water was still rising. But he had won himself a few more seconds, and he shot to the surface, grabbed another gasp of air, and sank back down to the lock. In his hands Harry was already testing the strength of the remaining spectacle arm, to see how easily it would bend.

Could it work? For the Great Train Escape, he had picked the padlock with a nail held between his teeth. He had picked the lock on the library door with a paper clip, and he had picked his way into the hotel manager's office with a fork. But what if the lock on the cage door was unusually difficult? What if the made-in-Peru spectacle arm was too weak to hold the shape? Even worse, it was almost impossible to see in the watery gloom, and Harry could hardly make out the lock's insides at all. Using a little guesswork, he twisted the spectacle arm into a new curve. It slid in and he probed the lock's levers, but gave up because his hand was trembling too much. His breath was out, and his heart was making his whole body shake. *Grab another breath and try again*, he decided, and he pushed for the water's surface.

Too late. The water had risen too high, and his face slammed against the cage bars. His lips strained upwards, but the rippling surface was too far away. He sank downwards, his heart throbbing, his legs, arms, hands losing their last traces of feeling. The water became darker, more blurry, as his eyelids flickered.

The Princess Moldo spectacle arm slid from his fingers. He hung there in the water, icy and black.

His eyes closed. He stopped moving.

*One . . . One . . . One last try . . .*

An eye opened. He peered down, and saw the spectacle arm, just vanishing into the gloom. His fingers twitched after it, but it was already gone. With a last quiver of strength, he turned himself in the water, reaching after it. Slowly, he rotated, until he was nearly upside down . . .

With the tip of his fingers, he caught it.

Still upside down, he saw the lock. It was just a few feet away. Feebly, he lifted the spectacle arm. He tried to angle it in, but it bumped against the keyhole's edges. Then it slid in. He tilted it, twisted it. He had to concentrate on keeping his numb hands moving, stopping them from falling limply away. His eyes were wide open, unblinking, but the water was growing darker and more blurry. He could hardly see at all.

But he could hear.

And, muffled by water, he heard . . .

. . . A CLICK.

The lock sprang open. Harry tugged the door, but it was stiff, so he had to tug again. It slid across, and he tried to squeeze through, but the gap was too narrow and he had to wriggle. He wondered if he had already died, if the whole experience of the last few seconds had just been the final flickers of his drowning mind—then a kick sent him racing upwards and he burst onto the surface. Air raced so fast into his lungs it was as if he had been punched, and he nearly sank back into the water with the shock. He struggled on, reached the stairs, and pulled himself up them, gasping, his hands still empty of feeling. Reaching the top, he slammed into a solid wall, the back of the mantelpiece, but he remembered the position of the switch on the other side and found the mechanism. He sprang it, toppled into Wesley's office, thudded onto the rug, and realized what a terrible mistake he had made.

Footsteps. Uneven footsteps, echoing up the corridor outside the office.

Harry tried to get up. His fingers arched on the rug, trying to push, but his strength was gone. The footsteps were closer now. *What a fool*, he thought, not to realize that Wesley or Arnold might return to the office. His escape had been for nothing, even with the help of his friends . . .

*His friends.*

'Harry!'

Arthur had slid out from behind the office door. Billie had thrown aside a curtain. They stared at him, but then they swung round in the direction of the footsteps. Arthur sprang towards the mantelpiece, and Harry heard the grind as it slid shut. He felt Billie's hands under his arms, tugging him up, and Arthur was helping her too, dragging him out through the office door. The footsteps were even louder, and Arnold's shadow slanted into view, but Billie flung open another door, bundled them into a cobweb-strewn dressing room, and silently closed the door behind them.

More footsteps. The sound of papers fluttering on Wesley's desk. Billie tweaked the dressing-room door open just a crack, and Harry saw the shape of Arnold, papers under his arm, standing in the doorway to Wesley's office. He was staring in the direction of the mantelpiece. A satisfied nod, the faintest waft of a chuckle, and the stage manager swung back off down the corridor. Harry waited until the shuffling footsteps were gone, completely gone. Then, he spluttered out the words that, from the moment he had seen his friends, had been trying to force their way out through his lips.

'I'm sorry . . . I'm sorry . . .'

Immediately, his voice gave out. His lungs still ached, his heart still pounded, and the effort of speaking nearly choked him. But nothing was going to hold him back. Gripping the dusty edge of the dressing-room counter, he gathered his breath, all the time aware of his two friends, staring at him.

'Pardon?' said Arthur.

'I'm sorry about not listening to you earlier, Artie . . .' His breath was back, and he struggled on, in between gasps. 'When you were trying to tell me all about the Princess Moldo plan . . . I should have listened, I know that now! Apart from anything else, you were right about what you said about having enough of that sort of thing in your life already . . .' He was still gasping, and he was dripping wet, but he forced himself to meet Arthur's eyes. 'Last thing you want is a friend who ignores you too. So I'm sorry, Artie, I really am . . .'

His voice gave out again. And for a while, nothing more was said, Arthur just stared at Harry across the dilapidated dressing room. But then the younger boy nodded, and adjusted his tie, and looked away.

'Fair enough,' he said.

'What about me?' said Billie, drumming her fingers on the counter.

'Well, obviously, I'm really sorry about that too.' Another gasp, but Harry found that his breath came back faster this time, which was fortunate, because Billie was looking straight at him. 'You're right, I should have gone along with the Princess Moldo business without interfering. In fact, I should have paid a lot more attention to you and Artie generally, I reckon.'

He swallowed. 'You were right earlier, Billie. Each of us, we're not so much, not on our own. Arthur's a rich boy who gets ignored, you're just a penniless street kid and as for me, well, no one was paying me and my tricks any attention until you two came along. But once we joined together . . .'

'Exactly,' said Billie.

'Besides, why wouldn't I want to listen to you? You're just as good at thinking up plans as I am! All those stories of the stuff you've got up to, Billie—that proves it, doesn't it? And you're good too, Artie—how could you not be, with all those books you've read! Come to think of it, both of you being here at the Wesley Jones Theatre proves just how good you are. I didn't say where I was going—how'd you work it out?'

'If you'd just stop talking, we might tell you.' Billie dropped into a rickety chair and swung her boots onto the dressing room counter. 'It was a pretty smart business— eh, Artie?'

'Absolutely.' Artie dropped into a chair too, a tiny smile beginning to curve on his lips. 'It wasn't that hard, to be honest. Number 47, that was the streetcar you jumped onto.'

'And we remembered you jumping onto the same number streetcar before, so we just looked up where the Number 47 went, and saw it was the Wesley Jones

Theatre.' Billie's boots swapped places. 'Pretty clever, yeah?'

'Brilliant.' There was no third chair, so Harry just stayed where he was, clinging to the wall. 'Just brilliant.'

'So we came right here and managed to break in easy enough. Sneaking up just now, we heard Wesley Jones, owner of this place, chatting to some thin guy about—'

'About a boy!' Arthur leaned back in his chair. 'About how they'd "dealt with him" and how he "wouldn't be trouble no longer"—it didn't sound good, Harry!'

'No, it did not,' Billie continued. 'Anyway despite everything you've done recently, Harry, we're still your pals, and someone has to look after you, so we thought we'd find out more—'

'We snuck up here to Wesley Jones's office and started searching for clues! And we were just starting doing that when the mantelpiece swung open and you came in!'

'Exactly. So that's what we've been up to. What about you?' Billie peered at her friend, and studied the water trickling from his clothes, the puddle spreading around his boots. 'Been swimming?'

Harry told them. He was still recovering, and so the first bit was a bit of a muddle, but he kept going, forcing out as many words as he could. He told them about Boris, about Herbie, about the terrible truth behind Wesley Jones's theatre—and he must have been making some sort of sense, because his friends were saying nothing at all, taking everything in. Harry saw Arthur's mouth fall open, and even Billie showed not the slightest sign of interrupting, and she stayed that way right up until when Harry reached the bit about stumbling back into the office and collapsing on the rug.

'He tried to kill you? Actually properly KILL you?'

'The Cruel Theatre of Wesley Jones!' Arthur whistled. 'Who would have believed it?'

'And who's gonna believe it even NOW?' Billie was up out of the chair, pacing the room, twiddling her thumbs behind her so fast that they seemed to propel her along. 'That's the trouble, Artie!'

*She's right.* Harry was still dripping wet, but he was feeling stronger now, and he could see what Billie was saying. Yes, he had discovered the terrible truth behind Herbie's disappearance. Yes, Wesley Jones had tried to silence him for ever, not one to take chances. *But that doesn't mean telling the world the truth about this terrible theatre is going to be easy,* he reflected—as Billie was continuing to point out.

'It'd have been fine if you'd got Herbie out—he could back us up. But he's still trapped here, isn't he?

He'll be too scared to say a word! Same for all the performers! So that leaves just us, a bunch of kids—and it's just like you said before, Harry, no one's going to take *our* word for it! Not the police, not anyone else! At most, someone might ask Wesley a few questions, but do you think he'll have any trouble thinking up something to cover his tracks? Not one bit! It's a hard one all right . . .' Her thumbs twiddled even faster. 'Mind you, I'm not saying it's impossible . . .'

*Definitely not impossible.* Leaning against the dressing room's crumbling wall, Harry realized that little bits and pieces of a plan were flying around his thoughts, waiting to be put together so that this business could be sorted out once and for all. They were getting clearer all the time, those bits and pieces, and yet he decided to ignore them completely, just for now. He felt his eyes narrow, and his teeth grit, with the concentration of doing so. Given everything that had happened recently, it seemed important that he approach things a bit differently this time, and he let his eyes open, and glanced down at his left fist, to remind himself why.

Knuckles white, it was still clutching the twisted remains of the Princess Moldo spectacles. Slowly, he turned to his friends, and spoke.

'Let's do this together, shall we?'

# Chapter 22

Harry hid in the backstage shadows, Billie squeezed next to him, Arthur huddled behind. Out on the stage, the evening show was underway, Bruno the Strongman just finishing his act, sloping towards the wings with a mournful expression. *But all the performers look miserable*, thought Harry—the Pearl-Diving Dancers, the Juggling Acrobats, the Man Who Told Jokes While Dressed as a Parrot. *Why wouldn't they, with nothing but a desperate future slaving at the Cruel Theatre Of Wesley Jones awaiting them?* Screwing his eye to the tiny hole in the backstage wall, he peered out at the audience, and listened to its excited muttering.

'Herbie Lemster! He's back and no one knows how!'

'The police never solved it! It's a darn mystery!'

'I was there that night! Vanished into a puff of smoke, he did!'

'Dark forces, that's what they say! It's the only explanation!'

The rumours raced about. They built in volume until they almost blotted out the applause that accompanied the next act, the Juggling Acrobats. The audience settled down to watch it, but it was clear from their faces, and the continued muttering, that they were thinking only of Herbie Lemster, due to appear at any moment.

'Wesley's plan's working nicely, ain't it, Harry?' Billie peered through another hole.

'Certainly is,' Harry muttered. 'Arnold's slapped up a few posters outside, announcing Herbie's return. Plus I saw Wesley wandering about the audience just before the show, chatting and laughing—'

'Getting the rumours started!' Arthur butted in. 'He's told the newspapers too—plenty of journalists in the audience, I saw them come in. All of New York talking about Herbie and now he's come back out of nowhere! Wesley isn't just going to keep his terrible theatre going, it's going to be more successful than ever and—'

'Pretty smart plan.' Billie swung round from her spyhole. 'But Wesley Jones ain't the only one who's cooked up one of *those*—is he?'

She pointed at the sheet of paper in Arthur's hands. It was covered with three different types of handwriting, all spiralling in different directions, a mass of scribbled words and diagrams. It had been Artie's idea that they each write their different ideas down, and the result was something of a mess, but it fitted, every last scribbling of it, onto one page, and Arthur was proudly holding it in his hands. Billie reached out, and took hold of a corner of it. Harry grabbed it too. It hovered there, gripped in their three hands.

'Let's just do it, shall we?'

They raced through the shadows. Unseen, they glided past Bruno, the Pearl-Diving Ladies, a couple of the Cossack Dancers, all looking as mournful as ever. Arriving in the corner of the backstage area, by the huge piece of wooden seaweed, Harry rooted through the collection of ropes, chose one, tossed it into Arthur's arms, and headed off with him into the dark. Hurrying through the gloom, he spotted the most mournful-looking figure of all, trudging towards the stage.

Herbie. What a broken figure he looked. His grey hair drooped, his body shivered, and his suit was still damp and creased after his time imprisoned in Wesley Jones's cage. Harry remembered the terror of the old magician down there, and he looked hardly less frightened now, tottering through the wings, forced to perform once again. A dreadful sight, made even more terrible by the sound of a familiar voice, wafting gleefully from the stage.

'Ladies and gentlemen, we come now to the main business of the evening! The miraculous return of Herbie Lemster, our resident magician!' It was Wesley Jones, out on the stage, the pink top hat twirling as he boomed out his announcement. 'Many of you may have heard of the strange events of last night! Purple smoke, an inexplicable disappearance! Sadly, ladies and gentlemen, I am unable to shed any light on the affair, it will be a mystery that will grip and baffle this city for years to come, I venture.' A wink over the hat's rim. 'What I can say is, however unexplained his dis-appearance, Herbie is with us once again! Puzzle for yourselves, if you will, about his vanishing. But here he is, ladies and gentlemen! HERE HE IS!'

The applause was tumultuous. The audience cheered, and there were even shrieks as the old magi-cian went shuffling on. Harry was deep in the backstage gloom, but he could still just make out the stage—and he had never seen anyone look so miserable as Herbie taking up his position, nor had he ever seen anyone as gleefully happy as Wesley Jones as he marched into the wings. Chuckling, the theatre manager handed his hat to Arnold, who was smirking and looked perfectly happy about the business too.

Harry shifted his gaze to Billie, as she wandered out of the shadows and strolled up to the two villains.

'Excuse me?' She propped herself casually against some scenery. 'Don't suppose you've seen a boy round here, have you? Harry's his name, and he's a good friend of mine—'

Arnold lunged for her and Billie was running as fast as she could. Harry watched her tiny outline, hurtling away from the wings towards him. Arnold and Wesley were close behind but Billie raced through the gloom, her glue-spattered smock flapping as she gathered speed. What would she call this latest adventure of hers, when she came to tell the story? *The Wesley Jones Theatre Dash*, maybe? Harry watched her hurtle right past him, vanishing through a doorway into the props room, which was where they had carefully agreed she should run.

Even though it was a dead end.

'You won't get out that way, kid!'

Harry saw Wesley and Arnold, their faces grinning as they closed in on the doorway. He heard Billie scrabbling about in the props-crammed room. *Caught in a trap.* But who was? Her or them?

'Ready, Harry?'

'Ready!'

A rope was pulled tight across the doorway, level with Arnold and Wesley's knees. Harry held one end;

the other was gripped by Arthur on the opposite side. The two men slammed onto the props room floor, and Billie skipped over them, not particularly seeming to mind as she trod on Wesley's hat, squashing it pancake flat, and on Arnold's hand, producing a high-pitched yell. She was out of the room. Arthur and Harry, still clutching either end of the rope, slammed and locked the door.

'All went rather smoothly,' Arthur said.

'Nice work,' Billie agreed.

'Ready for the next bit, Artie?' said Harry.

'I'll just finish off a few rewrites,' Artie muttered, flipping over the sheet of paper and jotting some more, as they hurried back towards the stage. Applause roared as Herbie completed the first part of his act, and Harry could see him out there, his frail arms holding up the glittering knives that had been magically hurled at him, his face staring sadly as the audience howled. A miserable sight. But, with a jab of his pencil, Arthur was ready, and Harry unhooked the rope that held the curtain, sending it thundering down. The audience gasped with dismay, and Arthur and Billie marched onto the stage, leaving Harry waiting in the backstage darkness.

'Ladies and gentlemen, I have an announcement to make!' This was Arthur's big moment, and Harry watched him leap to the front, the sheet of paper fluttering in his hand. 'Fear not, Herbie's act is not over! Indeed, it has only just begun! Never in your life will you have witnessed—'

'Who are you?'

'Get off the stage!'

'Kids! What're two kids doing up there?'

*A tricky start*, thought Harry. But his friends had expected that. And it wasn't as if anyone was actually going to stop them, was it? From his position in the wings, Harry glanced around, and saw the other performers standing there, too astonished to do anything, while all that could be heard of Arnold and Wesley was some far-away hammering on a door. Meanwhile, out on the stage, Billie was nudging Artie, keeping him going.

'Ladies and gentlemen, prepare yourself for the shock of your lives! You will not be seeing Herbie's usual tricks! No poisonous spiders and flowers! No bicycling over deadly spikes! No, what you are about to witness is more startling by far! For you are about to see with your own eyes, hear with your own ears . . .' Arthur yelled the last few words at the very top of his voice. 'The truth behind the disappearance of Herbie Lemster! A tale of trickery, malice, and attempted murder to boot!'

Silence. *Nicely timed*, Harry thought, and he saw that Arthur looked pretty pleased too, folding his speech up and sliding it into his pocket with a tap. A few more seconds went by and still not a sound from the crowd. Even before the show, they had been obsessed with rumours of Herbie's vanishing. *That'll be nothing compared to now*, Harry decided, and darted through a doorway, running up a corridor that ran parallel to the auditorium.

'If you want to find out more, follow us!' Billie's voice echoed through the theatre. Passing a doorway, Harry glanced back through it, and saw his friends leaping from the stage. Another doorway, and he saw the two of them running up the aisle through the audience, who seemed trapped in silence, gawping at them. But then Harry heard a seat thudding up, followed by another, and another. Behind his friends, he saw members of the audience, all around the auditorium, stumbling towards the aisle.

'The secret of Herbie's disappearance? Tell us!'

'What is it? I demand to know!'

'Is it dark magic? Like everyone says it is?'

'Follow them! Don't let them get away!'

Harry took off again. He slammed into the foyer, and flung open the door that led up to Wesley's office. Racing upstairs, he heard Billie and Arthur's voices echoing behind him, along with hundreds of other voices too, a thundering wall of shouts and gasps and demands for information. *They won't be disappointed,* he thought, as he flew along a final corridor, slammed into the office, rummaged under the mantelpiece shelf, and sent the marble bulk lurching to the side.

He leaped through into the dark. Flying down the spiral stairs, he splashed into the icy water. Over by the wall, he tugged at a lever, making the water swirl, and then he waded towards the cage. He slid the door open, and slammed it shut behind him. A flick of his wrist sent the key flying from the lock, plopping into the water, far away. Harry felt his heart throb with the memory of his last experience of this terrible device but ignored it. He grabbed the end of a rope that he had positioned ear-lier, running all the way over to the lever by the stairs, and tugged it. The lever clanked to the left and the cage began grinding down into the swirling black water again.

'Behold, we are in the office of Wesley Jones himself!' Harry heard Billie's voice, close now. 'The respectable theatre manager! But all is not as it seems!'

'Out of our way!'

The crowd was clattering down the stairs, the darkness echoing with their cries. Mouths fell open, eyes bulged, and a lady near the front fainted, but was picked up and carried along. The entire staircase groaned, as over a hundred people peered around the gloomy place, with its throbbing pipes, swirling water, and single flickering candle.

'What is this place?'

'Look at the speed of that water!'

'Who would build something like this?'

'In a theatre of all places?'

'What's that over there? It's . . . a cage!'

'It's MOVING!'

'Sinking, you mean!'

'And there's someone in it!'

'A BOY!'

The darkness shuddered with their screams. The crowd was in the water, surrounding the cage, yelling at it, pulling at its bars. Harry spotted Billie and Arthur in the water too, screaming loudest of all, all part of the plan to create the most panicked atmosphere possible. Harry saw the rigid faces, the screaming mouths. The cage kept grinding down. The water was up to his neck, but hidden beneath its surface his fingers were reaching for that snapped-off arm of the Princess Moldo spectacles . . .

'Save him! Save him!'

'Stop the machine!'

'Who put him in there? Who would do such a thing?'

'What about the theatre owner? It was his office up there, wasn't it?'

'Just get the boy out!'

'I can't! It's locked!'

'Stop it sinking someone! Stop it!'

'LOOK!'

The cage door slammed open. Harry shot up through the foaming water, gasping for air. Two more ladies fainted, collapsing on the stairs, but no one noticed, too astounded at the sight of Harry clambering out of the water and onto the top of the cage. They seemed astounded by the words too, that raced out of his dripping mouth.

'It's time for you to know the truth . . . about Wesley Jones!'

Again, the story flew out of him. The last time he had told it, he had been recovering in the cobweb-strewn dressing room, and it had been a bit of a muddle. But the words racing out of him now were far clearer. Carefully, precisely, he had been prepared by Arthur, who had jotted down exactly what he should say so the whole affair would be presented in the easiest way possible. Harry had memorized every word and, from the look of the audience's faces as he reached the speech's end, those words were having the desired effect.

'And so, Wesley Jones imprisoned me! He left me here to die! But I escaped! I escaped, and here I am now, to tell the truth of Herbie Lemster's disappearance—and of the Cruel Theatre of Wesley Jones!'

'Wesley Jones! Stage Manager Arnold! Find them!'

The water churned, the iron stairs shuddered, the crowd raced out of the dungeon. Harry jumped off the cage and was swept along by the jostling bodies, and he saw that the same thing was happening to his friends. Together, they hurtled along with the furious crowd, as it poured out into Wesley's office and surged back into the theatre, all the way to the props room where, Harry's speech had made clear, Wesley and Arnold had been so cleverly imprisoned.

'They've gone!'

'Smashed their way out!'

'Used a palm tree as a battering ram!'

The door hung off its hinges, and one of the larger props, a fake tropical plant, lay nearby, snapped in half. Standing around, were the various performers—Bruno the Strongman, the Cossack Dancers, the Juggling Acrobats, the Man Who Told Jokes—looking confused. But most confused of all was the small, frail figure, standing among them.

Herbie Lemster. His eyes were wide, taking in the scene before him. He was staring at the smashed-down door. He was staring at the crowd. His legs were weak, but his fellow performers kept him upright. When he spoke, it was clear he could hardly believe what he was saying.

'They have fled!' the old magician gasped. 'Just a minute ago! None of us knew what was happening! They smashed out through the door and raced up towards Mr Jones's office—but they came racing back down again when they heard you coming!' Bewildered, he pointed at the stage door, which was still rocking on its hinges. 'Ran off into the night! None of us could make head or tail of it . . .'

'Catch them! Bring them back!'

A section of the crowd broke away and swept out through the stage door. But Harry paid no attention to that. Instead, his gaze was fixed on Herbie. He was still unsteady on his feet, his face was still wearily wrinkled, and yet it seemed, from what he was saying, that he was finally starting to understand what had just happened.

'You mean to say . . . we're free?' Tears trickled down his face. 'Free from our dreaded owner and his terrible trapeze artist stage manager? Free of the Cruel Theatre of Wesley Jones? It's not possible! And yet . . . it is! Thanks to . . .'

The crowd gasped. Herbie had lifted a trembling hand, and for a moment it seemed as if he was about to perform some magical act. But instead, Herbie just extended a finger. Tears flooding, he faced the crowd, pointing in the direction of Harry and his friends.

'Thanks to these remarkable young people here! This boy! His friends too! They've set us performers free, ladies and gentlemen! FREE!'

The crowd was out of control. Hands gripped Harry and he rose into the air. Glancing across, he saw Billie being held aloft too, and Arthur. Then the throwing began, the hands beneath Harry and his friends powering them up into the air and catching them again, while the whole theatre throbbed with cheers. *Heroes, all three of us*, thought Harry, as the crowd threw them higher and higher. And Billie and Arthur's twists and turns in mid-air, he noticed, were every bit as spectacular as his own.

'We did it!' Billie waved at him, as she flew upwards again.

'We really did!' shouted out Arthur, his tie flying wildly around him.

'The Rescue Of Herbie Lemster!' Harry yelled back. 'It really is our most spectacular trick yet!'

He gazed around at the crowd's faces, whooping, cheering. And he noticed one face towards the back. White hair, white eyebrows, a pair of staring eyes. Harry thought nothing of it, but found himself looking at the face a second time, and a third time too.

*I've seen him before.*

He looked more closely. The man wore a pale, neatly tailored suit, and his hair was perfectly white, but otherwise there was no reason to pick him out. But Harry kept staring, as he flew up and down.

The tightrope walk at the Hotel Crosby. He had glimpsed him, that was all. A flash of paleness in the window pane, a face, white hair, a piercing stare. Harry couldn't be absolutely sure, but the longer he looked, the surer he became. It was the same man—but what was he doing here, in the crowd at the Wesley Jones Theatre? The Hotel Crosby was right on the other side of town—why would he be in both places, with just a few hours in between? As if this wasn't odd enough, why was the pale-suited man making notes? He was scribbling in a leather notebook, which appeared to have some sort of white bird on the cover. Even more strangely, wisps of white mist seemed to be rising from the pages . . .

Harry tried to look closer. But the crowd cheered even louder, and threw him up in the air so high that he spun right round. When he landed, he was facing in the other direction.

And when he looked back, the man in the pale suit was gone.

# Chapter 23

The man slid out through the stage door and hurried down the dark Manhattan street.

His pale suit fluttered as his long legs carried him along at speed. His steps were perfectly regular, and the soles of his polished shoes hit the sidewalk noiselessly, neatly.

The street was dark, apart from a gas-lamp's flickers. But the man's eyes tracked every one of those flickers, studying the complicated shapes of every shadow they threw. They swivelled about, checking the reflective surfaces of windows, metal railings, puddles on the sidewalk, for any information they might provide. The man was walking even faster now, but those eyes simply speeded up, monitoring the flying-past surroundings with even greater care.

He swung to the left. He marched up some steps and pushed through a heavy, gleaming door.

Those polished shoes snapped over a marble floor, a chandelier glittering above. The man spiralled up a mahogany staircase, his palm just touching the balustrade, skimming beside him. He reached the top, opened another door, and walked to a desk on which a telephone stood.

His hand lifted the receiver. On the underside of his wrist, a pulse twitched. As the receiver rose past the man's neck, a further pulse could be seen twitching just above his collar. The telephone crackled to life.

'A Candidate,' he said. 'Three of them, I now believe. I have been conducting my research with care . . .'

More crackling. The man listened, and spoke.

'I quite agree. Clearly, we need to test them. That is critical. We need to select an investigation suitable to their skills without delay and...'

The crackling went on for quite some time. Complicated pops and buzzes interweaved, and the pale-suited man's eyes narrowed, as if he was deciphering complex code. But at last the crackling ceased, and he spoke again.

'Very well. I shall begin the preparations.'

# Chapter 24

*Time to escape from Wesley Jones's deadly device once again.*

Harry stood before the cage. Hands tore through his clothes, removed his boots, explored his mouth, searching for the tiniest hint of anything that might assist him. The hands hoisted him up and dropped him into the cage. The lid clanged down, the key soared into the gloom. Harry saw faces in the darkness, hundreds of them, distorted with fear, thrill, glee. But he concentrated on Billie's face, pushing up to the bars.

'Ready?'

'Like always.'

A rope hoisted the cage upwards. Arthur stood at the front of the stage, his arms swirling as he addressed the crowd. Swinging round to the small cluster of invited audience members, he politely asked if the search they had just conducted had revealed anything suspicious. Heads shook. Arthur flung out an arm, and the cage, a little smaller than Wesley's original, swung over a water-filled vat. Harry tightened his grip on the bars, the audience bayed, but then their noise vanished as the cage plunged into the vat, and water engulfed Harry, the cage's locked lid solid over his head.

*Concentrate.*

His fingers flexed. His left foot rose. In between two of his toes, the earring was lodged. Billie had let it fall from her ear as their faces grew close, and the toes of Harry's left foot, stripped of sock and boot, had gathered it up. It was in his hands now, bending into shape, diving into the lock. Too bad about the Princess Moldo spectacles but the metal arms had weakened too much and, anyway, the earring was much smaller and easier to pass. The lock sprang loose, he clanged open the lid. Clambering out, he dropped down onto the stage and lowered himself in the usual bow, as Billie and Arthur ran to join him.

'Behold! He has escaped once more!' Arthur finished off his speech. 'Doomed to a watery grave! Yet he has survived to tell the truth about Wesley Jones!'

*The new trick.* The idea for it had hit all three of them at the same time. The whole of New York was talking about the amazing rescue of Herbie Lemster— why not let them see it unfold, night after night? As the applause roared, Harry took in the stage. To the left loomed a painted flat of Herbie's dressing room window, from which the disappearance itself was staged with a puff of purple smoke. Forty foot high, a rope spanned the stage, on which he re-enacted the walk into the Hotel Crosby and then there was the cage and water-filled vat, a practical way of staging the investigation's climax in Wesley Jones's deadly chamber. Best of all, there were Billie and Arthur, who helped him with every aspect of this dazzling show, Billie managing the tricks, Arthur narrating from his very own script. Regarding Arthur, there was something else too, something that had only been added to the show in the last couple of performances, but which was going down very well indeed.

'Behold the latest escape . . .' Arthur was shouting it out as grandly as he could. 'Of Harry HOUDINI!'

The new name. It had been suggested by that conversation with Arthur, which felt like such a long time ago. An invented name to catch the attention: half-borrowed from a famous French magician of the past, with a touch of Hungarian too. Harry liked it, so did his friends. Most importantly, the audience seemed to like it too.

'HOUDINI! HOUDINI! HOUDINI!'

The name thundered out of the auditorium's gloom. Harry bowed to the cheering audience again and, on either side of him, Billie and Arthur took bows too, and swapped places, Billie taking the central bow, then Arthur, then Harry again. The applause swelled, the curtain fell, and the three friends headed off into the wings.

'That new curtain call works well, I think.' Harry led the way up.

'You bet!' Billie snatched up her ukulele, and picked out a tune. 'Only fair we all get a turn!'

'Which fits in well with how things are these days at the Herbie Lemster Theatre, don't you think?' said Arthur, as they reached the top of the stairs.

A quick knock, and they swept in to the office. The marble mantelpiece was still there but new bolts fixed it to the wall and a fire crackled comfortingly in its grate. More comforting still was the sight, across the desk, of Herbie Lemster, writing in a ledger and sipping a cup of tea. His grey hair was neatly combed, he was wearing a brand new suit, and the wrinkles of his face were arranged in a cheerful expression as he greeted Harry and his friends.

'Come in! Make yourselves comfortable!'

'How's business, Herbie?' Harry dropped into a chair.

'Splendid! Your act in particular is going down tremendously well. Spectacular trickery! Although it's hardly surprising, given that you were taught by an expert.' Herbie winked, and pushed three envelopes across the desk. 'Mind you, all the acts at this theatre are impressive. That's why everyone gets their fair share of the takings.'

'No trouble taking over the ownership then?' Arthur enquired.

'How could there be? Legally, it still belongs to Jones but he and that trapeze artist stage manager aren't coming back any time soon. They're wanted by the police for extortion, blackmail, false imprisonment, and attempted murder. Along with various infringements of New York plumbing regulations.'

'Last I heard, they were in Mexico City, scraping together a living with a street theatre act.' Billie smiled. 'Arnold juggles tin cans, while Wesley tries to play a half-smashed-up saxophone.'

'A rotten act for two rotten fellows.' Herbie chuckled. 'Anyway, I just did a deal with a bank. They purchased the theatre on behalf of us performers and, given the publicity surrounding recent events, offered a very fair rate of interest too. As long as we manage it well, we'll own the place outright in just a couple of years! It'll be all of ours equally, although my fellow performers also suggested we paint my name on the front.' Herbie blushed. 'After all, why not take

advantage of the excitement regarding my famous disappearance, eh? Wouldn't you agree, Boris?'

'Of course, dear Mr Herbie! Of course!'

That familiar voice boomed across the office. Harry
swung round and saw the burly magician stooped over
a tiny table, stirring liquids in test tubes. Plumes of
orange smoke rose around his face, but his expression
was plain to see. Those tiny eyes twinkled, and a smile
curved under that long, thin nose.

'At last, my dream is true! No more lonely life on
the magician's road—I have found my home here,
with my oldest friend! Have I not, Herbie?'

'You have, dear Boris!' Herbie Lemster sprang
from his desk, and put an arm around the hefty figure.

'We must celebrate our good fortune, Herbie.
And we shall!' Boris lifted a test tube. 'In honour of
the occasion, I have invented a new Magician's Fire.
Orange version!'

A happy picture. Behind the two men, the mantelpiece stood, and it was lined with newly taken
photographs of the theatre's performers, the
Cossack Dancers, the Man Who Told Jokes, Bruno
the Strongman, and all the others, all in new outfits
and with cheery expressions. But cheeriest of all were
Herbie and Boris, reunited at last. Harry felt a smile
curve on his own face as he took in the happy pair, and

in particular the spindly shape of Herbie. *Herbie, who had started everything.* Down by his side, Harry's fingers were fluttering, as he remembered that very first meeting, in the middle of the New York winter, that trick with the flaming matches . . .

'Talking of magical powders and so on, Herbie . . .' Billie was trying to sound casual. 'I don't suppose you'd finally consider giving us a few clues about some of those other tricks you do? The Bicycling Over Spikes, perhaps? Spider Up Sleeve?'

'It would be useful.' Arthur chuckled. 'Harry never did work anything out that night. Obviously, I know he's meant to figure them out himself, part of the Game and all that. But a few hints would be most useful . . .'

'Would they indeed?' Herbie Lemster chuckled as he helped Boris mix the contents of the test tube. 'I'll think about it. But it strikes me young Harry's perfectly skilled at unmasking secrets already—he exposed the truth of Wesley Jones's doings, didn't he? Not to mention making a few other discoveries along the way, I hear.' He looked up. 'Not about magic perhaps—but important nonetheless . . .'

Those wrinkle-surrounded eyes gleamed at Harry. They flicked over to Arthur and Billie, and then back to Harry again. The old magician's expression was mysterious, but to Harry the remark he had made was perfectly clear, although not much else was, because just then Boris chuckled, tilted the test tube and, with a thundering explosion, the room filled with orange smoke, thick and swirling. Billie waved at the plumes, Arthur wheezed, and Harry stumbled to the window, but by the time he had rattled it up and cleared the air, the two magicians had gone. *So much for clues about tricks.* He dropped back into his chair, and counted the money inside the brown envelope Herbie had given him.

*How things have changed.* Harry lifted a hand, and examined it through the smoke. Traces of boot polish stain could be seen on the fingertips but that was all. Strange, to think of the job he had once had, lugging that shoeshine box around in an attempt to earn a few cents. The shoeshine box was long ago abandoned, and he had changed his lodgings too, the rather dilapidated boarding house of Mrs Mack left behind. *And it's not just me who's finding things a bit different.*

'How'd you think Mawkin's Glue Factory is managing without you, Billie?'

'Don't ask me, never gone near the place, and I'm not planning to either.' Billie flicked through the contents of her brown envelope too. 'I'm done with gloop-stirring. Same goes for all the other crummy work I've done—floor-sweeping, garbage-picking, and all the rest . . .'

'You really have done some terrible jobs, Billie.' Arthur nodded thoughtfully.

'It's true. Come to think of it, nothing much about the road from New Orleans has been that easy, what with escaping from orphanages, trying to jump trains, and generally having to scratch a living together any way I could. Still, like I always say, it's not the sticky situations that matter, it's how you get out of them.' Another tap of the brown envelope, and there was a particularly wide grin on Billie's face, even by her standards. 'And I don't think I've ever managed to wriggle my way out as spectacularly as this. Ending up in a real, proper job, doing stuff I actually like, and making some proper cash too!'

'You're right, we're on to a pretty good earner,' Arthur chipped in. 'Not that I personally need the money, which is why I give most of it to the two of you.' He pulled two handfuls of notes out of his envelope and handed one to Harry, the other to Billie. 'Although I am going to keep a bit back, if that's all right, to help fund my new Special Membership cards to the Boston, Paris, and London Libraries. In case I need books that aren't in New York? They'll mail them right to me, you know—might be handy if we get round to thinking up some new tricks for the show?'

'Absolutely, Artie . . .' Harry hesitated, remembering something. 'By the way, the boarding school plan. Went off well?'

'Certainly did!' Arthur fished in his pockets. More paper ribbon spilled out, along with various envelopes and a book, which he thumped onto the table. *Techniques of Famous Forgers*, the title said. 'So, that letter we snatched, way back, was just the beginning. Ever since, Father's servants have been writing letters to the school, and the school's been busily writing back, but none of those letters have ever arrived, because I've intercepted them, obviously. Picked up the school's ones as they fell through the letter box, grabbed the servants' ones just before they were posted.' He reached into another pocket and pulled out a little twisted length of metal. 'This pick you made me for the letter box outside my house came in handy, Harry.'

'No problem.' Harry smiled.

'So anyway, instead of the servants and the school getting the letters they expect, they're getting ones specially forged by me.' As Arthur tapped the book, Harry saw that on his forehead there was no sign of that shadowy kink at all. 'The very last letter from the school, in fact by me, was opened by the servants just yesterday, and it described all the final arrangements.'

'Which were?'

'A cab called at the house just this morning. I boarded it with all my luggage, looked mournful and all that. But instead of taking me 452 miles away, like Father wanted, it brought me right here.' Arthur jerked a thumb at a couple of trunks, piled in the corner of Herbie's office. 'I thought I might make myself at home in one of the dressing rooms? Until the end of term, that is?'

'What about the school?' asked Billie. 'Won't they think it's odd when you don't arrive?'

'Not really because the last letter they got announced Father had changed his mind, and was sending me to a slightly cheaper school down the road from them instead. They'll be so annoyed they'll just throw the letter in the bin. As for Father himself, I doubt he'll find out any time soon—not least because he's only just set off on yet another business trip. Back to London, this time.'

'London?'

'He'll be gone nearly six months. So it looks like he'll be carrying on paying no attention to me, boarding school or not.' A frown, but it was a very slight one. 'I know, it's a strange business. But the truth is, I've pretty much got used to it these days. Is it really such a bad thing, him wanting me out of his way? When it ends up with him accidentally having me sent to a place like this, where I can spend as much time as I like, doing the best job in the world?' The frown was gone and in its place was a grin just as big as Billie's. 'Not to mention doing it with the best friends in the world too, eh?'

'Absolutely, Artie,' said Harry.

He watched his friends. Billie was nodding at what Arthur had said too, and had reached across and taken hold of his hand. Harry reached out, and took hold of the other one. Arthur smiled, and Harry realized that, if he leaned forward, he could just reach across and grab Billie's spare hand too. He did so, and for a moment the three of them sat like that, the fire beneath Wesley Jones's mantelpiece warming them with its flickering glow. *Yes, things have turned out pretty nicely*, Harry reflected . . .

*And we've only just got started.*

Releasing his friends' hands, leaning back, he thought about what Arthur had said just now, about researching new tricks. *Good point.* Thrilling though the Wesley Jones cage trick was, audiences would grow bored of it eventually, and new tricks would have to be devised, even more spectacular, even more death-defying. *But that won't be so hard*, Harry thought, feeling the warmth of the fire, and glancing across at his friends.

*Not as if I'm on my own.* Settling back in his chair, he started wondering what the next tricks would be . . .

'Master Harry? This just handed in for you at stage door.'

It was Bruno the Strongman. He was standing in the doorway, holding up an envelope. Harry rose from his chair, and trod across the rug, his boots still warm. He took the letter, and opened it, as Bruno shuffled away. A sheet of paper, pale green in colour, was inside. Burned into the bottom left corner, a symbol of a bird surrounded by black. And the letter's words were just as curious.

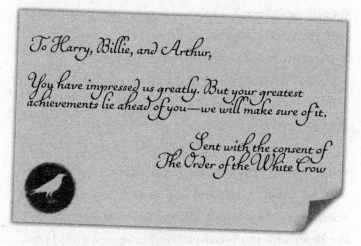

To Harry, Billie, and Arthur,

You have impressed us greatly. But your greatest achievements lie ahead of you—we will make sure of it.

Sent with the consent of
The Order of the White Crow

'The Order of the White Crow?' Arthur peered over Harry's shoulder.

*'We will make sure of it . . .'* Billie inspected the letter too. 'What's that supposed to mean?'

Harry said nothing. He just let Billie slide the pale green paper out of his hands, and headed for the window. *Just handed in at the stage door.* The sash was still open, and he leaned right out of it, and immediately remembered the tightrope walk into the Hotel Crosby, along with being thrown into the air by the ecstatic crowd, just a few days ago.

There he was. The man in the pale suit. The one he had glimpsed ten storeys up, the one who had written in the notebook as the crowd cheered. He was standing just a short distance down the street, staring directly up at Herbie Lemster's office window. And he stayed like that, staring, as Harry felt a strange twitching sensation in the fingers of his right hand.

He held them up. Their tips were smeared with a pale green dust. Looking closer, he saw that the greenness seemed to have become part of the skin, and that traces of it could even be seen underneath the skin too, dissolving into the pinkness of his fingers. But he couldn't look at his hand any longer, because his legs were feeling weak, and he needed it to grip the wall. He heard two thuds behind him.

Unsteadily, he swung round. He saw Billie sprawled on the rug, Arthur collapsed into a chair. Both of them were unconscious, their heads lolling, their bodies limp. The pale green letter stood upright, pinched between Arthur's finger and thumb. Harry took a step forward but his legs were even weaker and his knees slammed into the rug. He crawled to his friends. They were still breathing. They almost looked quite peaceful as they lay there, sound asleep.

The door opened. Harry watched it, and tried to look up, but his head was too heavy. He saw a pair of polished shoes, and the hems of some pale suit trousers, step into the room. They crossed to a point just a short distance away from him.

'Your greatest achievements do indeed lie ahead of you,' a voice said. 'You'll discover more shortly, when you wake up.'

Harry tipped forward onto the rug. He landed right next to the polished shoes. He saw his own face, reflected back to him in the gleaming leather. It was curved, out of shape. Who was this man? What was his purpose? Most importantly, what did he mean by 'greatest achievements'? Harry felt those strange little twitches quivering through his body again, and his heart pounded, as he readied himself for whatever lay ahead . . .

But—for the time being—his eyes flickered shut.

And he stopped seeing anything at all.

*To be continued . . .*

Photo: © Catherine Allerton

# About the Author

Simon Nicholson grew up in Raynes Park, London. He worked in theatre for a while before starting to write stories, mainly for children. Since then, he has written plays, books and over a hundred episodes of children's television series, and has been nominated for BAFTA and RTS awards. He lives in Winchester with his young family—and lots of books about Houdini.

'Harry's adventures will continue in
**THE DEMON CURSE.**
Coming soon . . .'

'Read on for an exclusive
extract of
THE DEMON CURSE...'

# One

Harry woke up. Or, at least, he thought he did.

Blackness, everywhere. He closed his eyes, and then forced them open, but it made no difference. Only the flutter of muscles in his face told him that he was opening and closing his eyes at all. He tried to move, but his legs, arms, and head were jammed. He fought, but his body stayed trapped, and the effort made him gasp as he tried to suck in air.

*Breathe.* His heart pounded, blood throbbing in his veins. The air around him was hot and stale, and when he drew it in, his body just ached for more. His head spun, and he felt a prickling sensation in his fingers, spreading into his hands. *Desperate for oxygen.* He sucked in another useless breath, but the sensation kept spreading. *Concentrate. Stay calm.*

His left hand swivelled slightly at the end of its wrist. His prickling fingers roamed about, exploring. He was in some sort of box. Its sides were rigid, holding his body, but his fingertips detected a thin lining. *Silk, perhaps?* Harry's heart beat harder and his breathing sped up, pain jabbing in his lungs like a knife. He gathered his mouth into a tiny hole, and forced himself to breathe through that. *Make the oxygen last.* Angling his hand, he let his fingertips creep along the lining of the box, until they found something hard, square, and metal.

*The inside of a lock.*

Harry forced the remaining air out of his lungs. His body fought, trying to cling on to every wisp of breath, but he pushed it all out so that his shoulders sunk and his ribs caved. In that tiny released space, he managed to swivel a leg upward just slightly, until the boot was braced against the box's inside. He breathed back in, and felt the box tighten around him. But his boot was in position, his leg hinged at the knee. His lungs ached, his head spun from lack of air, but he managed to kick, hard, and the box gave, just a little. Two cracks of light flashed briefly on either side of its lock. Harry's hand angled in a new direction, his fingers pushing through the lining's stitching, searching for what he needed.

He found it, just a couple of inches away. A sturdy metal staple, fastening the lining in place. He wriggled his fingernail beneath it, levered it up, and spun it in his fingers, straightening it. Harry braced his leg again, and kicked even harder. The cracks of light widened, and Harry's leg held the lid like that, muscles shaking. He squeezed two fingers through the gap, the staple gripped between them, as the edges of the crack bit into his flesh.

The edges bit deeper. The muscles of his leg were giving way, and the darkness of the box filled with hissing as his breathing grew even faster. He realized that his fingers and hands were no longer prickling, that a cold numbness was taking hold instead. Need air . . . His head spun again, and he saw visions dance in the blackness—a locked suitcase with two fingers prodding out of it, pale and weak, a little straightened-out staple falling away from them onto the ground . . .

A last shudder of strength in his leg. The gap widened, and his fingers wriggled out further. Through the numbness, he could just feel the shape of the staple, gripped between a finger and thumb. It was there, he knew it, and he angled it towards where the keyhole would be.

He thrust the staple in. He felt it bump against the lock's innards. He pushed an ear against the inside of the box, and listened to the noises: a spring stretching, a latch grinding. He could feel nothing at all in his fingers now as he moved them about, but he could hear the sounds, allowing him to go about his work.

*Click.* A latch fell into place. *Click.* Another one. Harry's boot pushed even harder, widening the crack, allowing his hand to reach further, his fingers to re-angle the staple one more time . . .

*Click.*

The box sprang open and the cracks became a blaze of light. Harry toppled out, and fell onto a shuddering wooden floor. Everything was shaking—the cushioned seat next to him, the wood-panelled walls. Harry blinked in the brightness, and looked up at a trembling iron rack, on which was a torn-open silk-lined packing case. *A railway carriage compartment.* He took in the sliding door, the fan rotating on the ceiling. Then he saw the window and flung himself at it, pulling up the lacework blind, pushing down the sash, and sucking in deep draughts of air.

A river blurred past, followed by a tangle of palm trees. The air felt warm and moist. His gasps slowed, his head stopped spinning, the feeling crept back into his skin. Harry looked down at his hand and saw, still gripped between his fingers, the straightened-out staple. The corners of his mouth curved slightly upwards. Turning away from the window, he pocketed the staple, and couldn't help putting a foot forward to perform a small bow. *Sheer habit,* he thought.

But then he heard the voices. He snapped upright again.

'Mmmpf . . .'

'Get me out . . .'

For the first time Harry noticed the iron rack on the *other* side of the compartment. He saw what was stacked on it—two more suitcases. He was up on the cushioned seat, his heart pounding again. Struggling noises drifted from the suitcases, along with muffled voices, getting weaker. Harry's hands shook as he fumbled in his pocket for the staple. *Hurry.* Pulling the staple out, he forced it into the first suitcase's lock.

'Hang on!' His voice cracked. 'It's me! I'll get you out—'

'Harry?' a voice cried out. The case on the left jolted. 'Is that you?'

'Quick . . . ' The voice from the other case was faint. 'Help me . . .'

The first lock sprung, Harry threw open the lid, and a girl toppled out. She had dark skin and tightly curled hair, and was wearing a scruffy factory smock. Harry managed to grab her as she fell, so that she bounced safely onto the cushioned seat below.

'Artie . . .' She sprawled there, gasping. "You've got to get Artie out too . . .'

Harry went to work on the second lock. A few seconds later a boy in a tweed suit fell out, thudding onto the cushioned seat next to Billie. Harry collapsed down between them and, for the second time, tried to get his breath back.

'What's going on?' the girl spluttered.

'Don't worry about that for now, Billie.' Harry grabbed her arm. 'Are you all right?'

'I think so . . . Good thing you rescued us. Reminds me of the time I was locked in a cupboard by the head chef of that hotel kitchen I worked in, back in Chattanooga—did I ever tell you about that?' Billie managed a smile, and then stared up at the suitcase on the opposite rack. 'How did you get yourself out, anyway? Tricky stuff, even by your standards.'

'I'll tell you later.' Harry turned to his other friend. 'Hang in there, Artie, you'll feel better soon.'

'I know . . . I could breathe in there but only just . . . It'll take a while for my blood to re-oxygenate completely . . .' Arthur loosened his tie, and pulled in another deep breath. 'But where are we? I think it's safe to say we're not in New York anymore.'

He stumbled over to the window. Harry and Billie joined him, gripping the windowsill and taking in the scene. Palm trees blurred past under a hot grey sky. The train curved and raced alongside a huge river, with a rippling brown surface that glittered in the sun.

'Definitely not New York,' Billie muttered. 'Palm trees, that's the big clue.'

'I'd say we must be two hundred miles south at least, given the palms and the high temperature.' Arthur's voice had steadied, his English tones neat and precise. 'I can't make head or tail of this. Last thing I properly remember, we were back in the theatre in New York helping Harry with his spectacular escape act and—'

'And then that letter was delivered, and we opened it.' Billie's eyes narrowed. 'That letter we read, all three of us—

and a few seconds later we were flat on the floor, all three of us, collapsing in some kind of drugged sleep.' Her eyes narrowed even more, and she pointed. 'That letter, which is still in your pocket, Harry, RIGHT THERE.'

Harry looked down and flinched. There it was, a folded piece of pale green paper, poking out of his jacket pocket. Arthur was already holding out a handkerchief, and Harry used it to gingerly pull the letter out. He too thought back to that moment, the three of them sitting in the theatre office. He remembered the act the three of them had just performed, full of the usual tricks involving razor-sharp knives, handcuffs and fire, and finishing with the most spectacular stunt of all, which involved him escaping from a small iron cage that had been plunged deep into a vat of water. *Thrilling stuff*, Harry thought, with another smile. Then he focused on the letter again.

'There was some sort of dust on the paper, which came away on our fingertips—now I think of it, I remember that too.' Arthur had taken a magnifying glass from his pocket, and was peering through it at the letter. 'Gone now, by the looks of it. Still, it certainly was powerful—knocked us out cold.'

'It's not just the paper we need to think about—what the letter actually says. That's pretty odd too,' muttered Harry, reading it one more time.

*To Harry, Billie, and Arthur,*

*You have impressed us greatly. But your greatest achievements lie ahead of you—we will make sure of it.*

*Sent with the consent of*
*The Order of the White Crow*

'The Order of the White Crow . . . ' Arthur frowned. 'Anyone got the faintest idea what that might be?'

'Nope—in fact, there's not a single bit of that letter that makes much sense, if you ask me,' Billie said. 'This sure is a mystery . . . Reminds me of the time I woke up and discovered I was tied up in the hold of a shrimp-boat off South Carolina, been press-ganged into another crummy job obviously, but it didn't take me long to escape and— WATCH OUT!'

Billie flung herself back against the compartment wall, and Arthur did the same. Harry took care to hold his breath, and extended his arm, so that he was staring at the letter from as far away as possible. Beneath the handwriting, whitish wisps floated from the page and more words appeared. Harry carried the letter to the window, where the breeze snatched the wisps away, leaving only the words.

P.S. Congratulations. If you are reading these additional remarks, then you are successfully launched on your mission, and it is safe to reveal more. Regarding the suitcases, we apologize, but secrecy is vital, and so we had to smuggle you out of New York entirely unseen. Concealed air holes were drilled, a convenient staple was left near Harry's hand for when the drugs wore off—we expected you managed the rest. Now, you no doubt wish to be told about our organization and its purpose? Perhaps it is simplest to say this: that it exists to unmask and defeat evil-doing wherever it may lie, and that it seeks to recruit those capable of helping that noble cause. Prepare yourselves for your first investigation . . .

# Five ways to continue the thrills!

# The Dangerous Discoveries of Gully Potchard

## Julia Lee

An unlikely hero, a wild chase,
and a surprising twist of fate . . .

£6.99
ISBN: 978-0-19-273370-2

# Young Knights of the Round Table

## Julia Golding

Under threat. Out of Time.
Pure Magic.

£6.99
ISBN: 978-0-19-273222-4

## Destination Earth
### Ali Sparkes

Ten days to get here.
Ten days to wipe us out . . .

£6.99
ISBN: 978-0-19-273344-3


## Charlie Merrick's Misfits in Friends, Fouls, and Football
### Dave Cousins

One boy, his misfit football team, and their unlikely journey to World Cup fame.

£6.99
ISBN: 978-0-19-273659-8

# Treasure Island
## Robert Louis Stevenson

Set sail on a swashbuckling
adventure . . .

£4.99
ISBN: 978-0-19-273745-8